"I'll give you the kiss," Callie promised, "but only when I'm good and ready."

Jack's confusion grew.

Tightening her arms around his neck, she pulled herself up and said in a throaty murmur, "Until then, you have to be polite."

"Polite?" he managed to whisper, his attention caught elsewhere. Her lush, hard-tipped, satin-clad breasts now hovered before him, eye level.

He felt his temperature rising. Heat engulfed him.

"Don't even think about it, Jack." Her whispered command stopped him, and her elbows trapped his hands on their slide up her slender rib cage.

"Before you make a move," she whispered, gazing at him with heated sensuality, "you'll have to say 'Callie, may I?'"

He stared at her, too stunned to think clearly, let alone reply.

"I might give you my permission." She tilted her head judiciously. "Then again—" her breasts brushed close enough for the body-heated satin to whisper across his face "—I might not."

Dear Reader,

You may remember Jack Forrester from my first book in the BEDSIDE MANNERS series, *Say "Ahhh..."* (April '99, Temptation #726). If so, you know he's not your typical orthopedic surgeon. As wild as he is, though, rest assured he's met his match in Callie.

Callie's relationship with Jack Forrester has always been somewhat stormy. And she should have known better than to think she could take care of business in Moccasin Point and get out unscathed. Instead, she finds herself swept up in an emotional tempest as powerful as any hurricane that ever hit the Florida coast.

Oddly enough, though, Jack's passions don't seem centered around the lawsuit at all...but around Callie. He's determined to win her over to his side. Business be damned. His motives are purely personal.

Hope you enjoy their skirmish! And I'd love to hear from you personally. You can write to me c/o P.O. Box 217, Auburn, GA 30011.

Donna Sterling

P.S. In November, look for *The Daddy Decision*, my contribution to Temptation's 15th Anniversary Celebration!

TEMPERATURE'S RISING
Donna Sterling

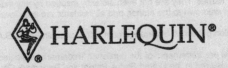

HARLEQUIN®

TORONTO • NEW YORK • LONDON
AMSTERDAM • PARIS • SYDNEY • HAMBURG
STOCKHOLM • ATHENS • TOKYO • MILAN • MADRID
PRAGUE • WARSAW • BUDAPEST • AUCKLAND

I dedicate this book to Joe and Dee, my mom and dad. You
truly are the "wind beneath my wings."

I'd like to thank my writer friends for their critiques:
Anne Bushyhead, Jacqui D'Alessandro, Susan Goggins,
Carina Rock and Ann White. For technical advice, I thank
Dr. Ed White, Dr. George Coletti, Linda from the Atlanta
Allergy Clinic, and my cousin, Ruth Zimmerman, nurse
extraordinaire. Your help was most appreciated.

ISBN 0-373-25838-0

TEMPERATURE'S RISING

Copyright © 1999 by Donna Fejes.

1

SHE HOPED IT wasn't an omen.

As Callie Marshall waded through warm, murky puddles in her expensive high-heel pumps, she thought about the Mercedes her sister had insisted she borrow to bring across an authoritative, I-mean-business image to the hometown folks who might otherwise receive her as the wayward teen she'd been twelve years ago.

The Mercedes now sat a mile behind her in the dense Florida foliage, bumper-deep in wet sand.

When the hell had Gulf Beach Road turned into a car-eating bog? She'd driven too far down the narrow sandy lane to hike back to the paved highway. If memory served, the beach and its private cottages should be closer.

Or so she hoped.

Sweat trickled between her breasts and dampened her white silk blouse as the Florida heat visibly steamed around her. At least she'd had the foresight to leave her panty hose and suit jacket in the car. She'd left her cell phone, too. The connection had been too weak for anyone to understand a word she said.

Gritting her teeth in frustration, Callie trudged between giant water oaks and palms, ropelike vines, glimmering spiderwebs and ghostly beards of black Spanish moss. The sweet, cloying scent of tropical foliage and fresh decay mingled with the tang of sea air.

The dense gloom hummed, shrieked and buzzed around her.

She'd known as a kid to avoid these woods during summer. After all, Moccasin Point hadn't been named for Indian shoes but for a noteworthy element of its wildlife. Water moccasins.

She swore she heard slithering in the bushes beside her and quickened her pace. Just as she began to worry that she'd grossly misjudged the distance to the beach, a tunnel of light opened ahead. Relief washed through her in strong, reviving currents. Squaring her shoulders, she plunged onward.

Dimness soon gave way to the golden sunlight of late afternoon. Lifting her face to the cool gulf breeze, she stepped onto firm malt-colored beach. Seagulls swooped with playful screeches in the azure sky. Gray-green waves crashed and foamed against the shore, where seashells glistened like treasures. The tranquil, wild beauty filled her with intense appreciation and a sudden nostalgic ache.

She used to belong here.

For an instant, she expected to see a ragtag group of barefoot kids running toward her from the boat docks or the sand dunes, led by a strong, fair-haired boy with sun-browned skin and a flashing white smile that usually meant mischief was afoot.

Jack.

He'd been her pal. Her accomplice. Her wild, fun-loving comrade at arms.

A sweet, sharp ache pierced her, and she cursed herself for it. She wouldn't think about Jack Forrester now. At least, not in any fond way. She'd have to deal with him soon enough. She wasn't looking forward to it.

As she turned toward the distant cottages, determined to concentrate on the business at hand rather than bothersome memories, a stirring in the palmetto bushes stopped her.

Her heart stood still. Two reptilian eyes peered at her from very near ground. They looked too big for a snake.

A beast slithered out from the brush. *An alligator.*

In dry-mouthed disbelief, Callie took one cautious step backward. Even when she'd been a kid, alligators were few and far between on this northern Florida peninsula. She'd seen them crossing the highway at times and glimpsed a few in the culverts and ponds, but she'd never been confronted with one, up close and personal.

The huge, lizardlike creature crawled forward. An alarm sounded in Callie's head. Gators usually fled from humans. Forward behavior meant they were hungry. Looking for a meal.

As fear squeezed the breath out of her, she noticed a scrap of orange fabric dragging behind the gator's short front legs. A shred of clothing from a previous victim, maybe?

Courage deserted her. In a blur of terror, she fled down the beach, her heart hammering. She'd grown up hearing grisly gator tales of mutilation and death. She wasn't ready to die.

Awkward in her high heels, she stumbled in the sand, highly aware that the gator kept easy pace beside her in the saw grass. With a terrified sob, she kicked off her soggy leather pumps and ran to a nearby cedar boathouse. As she leaped onto its stairway, she slipped and fell against a wooden rail.

Pain shot through her. Holding her injured side, she threw open the door and rushed into a dim, musty room. Slamming the door, she leaned against it and fervently prayed that the gator couldn't break through it.

A few heart-skidding moments passed. Her erratic pulse and frantic panting gradually subsided enough for her to think. She seemed to be safe for the moment. But what the hell should she do now?

She looked wildly around her, hoping for inspiration. The afternoon sun barely filtered through small dusty windows on the back wall. The redolence of dried shells, sea brine and diesel fuel permeated the air, a smell that brought back vague but comforting memories of her childhood.

She seemed to be in a large storage room at the rear of the boathouse. Old man Langley's boathouse, she believed it was, if it hadn't changed hands in twelve years.

Maybe she could signal for help. But how? As she searched for a way to do it, a noise caught her attention—a distant purring from out in the gulf. The sound grew steadily louder and she recognized it as a motor. An incoming boat!

She almost cried in relief. Help would soon be here, or at a nearby boat slip.

In moments, the floor and walls vibrated with the roar of an engine, and she realized the boat had pulled into this very boathouse. The engine sputtered into silence, and soon footsteps thudded up the plank.

Callie realized then that the newcomer was also in danger. Reports of vicious gator attacks again flashed through her mind. As the footsteps neared, she flung open the door to warn whoever was approaching. But before she could utter a word, a huge, solid body charged into her and slammed her against the interior wall of the boathouse, pinning her there with iron-strong arms and a muscled chest.

She struggled to catch her breath.

A man, she dazedly realized. A large, powerful man with angry brown eyes, golden hair and a jagged scar slashed across one cheek. He looked like a vengeful, mythical sea god rising up to slay her.

He didn't slay her, though. He merely held her against the wall and gaped at her as if she'd stunned him.

She gaped back, thoroughly stunned herself—and not only because of his attack. Despite the savage scar, angry scowl and caveman brutality, she recognized him.

Jack Forrester.

Of all people…Jack Forrester!

The surprise was enough to keep her breathless, even without the muscled forearm lodged against her windpipe.

"What the hell are you *doing*, lady?" he finally thundered, again invoking the image of an angered god. Even in the dimness of the boathouse, his hair glowed like muted sunshine and the strong, clean lines of his face radiated virility and power. "Don't you know I could have killed you?"

Oh, she knew.

"Let me go," she silently mouthed.

He immediately lowered his arm from her throat and backed away. His high-powered stare kept her pinned to the wall just as effectively.

She gulped in huge, blessed drafts of air, feeling dizzy, weak and shaken. He'd called her *lady*. He obviously hadn't recognized her. The idea both pleased and annoyed her. She liked having the upper hand, but how could he have forgotten her when she would have known him a hundred years from now?

Deciding to hold on to her slim advantage for as long

as possible, she swallowed the sardonic retort that had
risen to her lips. Might as well strike the right note with
him from the start—distant and polite. Anything but
familiar.

"Sorry I startled you," she said, her throat tight from
the shock of the attack. Reluctantly she noted that he
was even more handsome than he'd been as a teenager.
His face, with its new jagged scar, a five-o'clock
shadow and laugh lines around his amber-brown eyes,
held a more rugged appeal.

She wondered how he'd earned that scar. A fight,
probably, or some macho stunt. She wasn't surprised
to see the scar.

His body, always athletic and trim, had filled out
into a well-honed, manly physique. Faded jeans
molded to long, corded thighs and legs. An army-
green T-shirt stretched across a powerful chest—wide
and muscle hard, as she knew from having been
crushed beneath it.

He was too damn attractive for the good of woman-
kind. Whose heart, Callie wondered, was he breaking
now? He'd cut his teeth on her sister's.

Resentment she'd thought long buried flared once
again. Coolly she explained, "I may have saved your
life."

"Saved my life?" The Southern-soft voice was
deeper than she remembered and provoked a curious
weakening of her knees. She couldn't afford that. She
couldn't afford a weakening of any kind.

She raised her chin. "That's right. You see, there's
an—" Her words broke off and her eyes widened.
"The door!" she cried in renewed panic. "Shut the
door!"

Jack Forrester frowned, but obligingly pushed the
door closed, his gaze never leaving her face.

With every muscle in his body still tense from the adrenaline rush of being startled into a defensive attack, Jack struggled to make sense of what she was saying.

He was having a hard time of it.

Little wonder in that. He'd been strolling along after a day of fishing, wondering what diversion might keep him occupied for the evening—whether to drop in on a party or start one of his own—when a form had lunged at him.

The shock of it seemed to be stopping his mind from forming coherent thoughts. Or maybe it was the sheer surprise of having the breath knocked out of him by a pair of dusky green eyes. Something about them stirred him in a very personal way.

He felt oddly dazed.

Who was she?

She smelled like sunbaked wildflowers and clean, fresh, feminine sweat, as if he'd already engaged her in a long, hot bout of lovemaking. The idea, once in his head, wouldn't leave him. She'd felt soft, slender and incredibly *right* beneath him. He could still feel her womanly curves imprinted against his chest and thighs.

"My God, the door was open all that time," she murmured, more to herself than to him, crossing her hands over her heart. Her soft, throaty voice sounded vaguely familiar. "We could have been devoured!"

"Devoured," he repeated.

Her face, he suddenly realized, also seemed familiar. Why? He doubted he'd met her before. He would have remembered. Just looking at her now made him feel as if a freight train had thundered through his chest. A man tended to remember something like that.

Hooking his thumbs into the pockets of his jeans, he

took in the rest of her. Short, dark hair glimmered around her face in feathery disarray. Sand sparkled on her short-sleeved blouse. Silk, he believed it was. Damp, white silk. It clung to small, pert breasts in the most provocative way.

Heat kindled in his loins, and his body reacted. Shaken by his own response, he forced his gaze downward to a slim gray skirt that came to just below her knees; shapely calves; slender bare feet.

Business clothes, he realized, fixing his attention on something he could objectively consider. She was wearing business clothes. On the beach. In his boathouse.

Had she said something about being *devoured*?

"There's an alligator out there," she divulged, "and he's acting hungry." Her serious, gray-green eyes remained on his as she pressed her slender back to the door. "He chased me down the beach!"

That caught his attention. Finally she was making sense. Or maybe his thought processes had simply started working again. "An alligator. My God, no wonder you're shaken up. And then I had to go and tackle you. Damn, I'm sorry. I even yelled at you, didn't I? I really am sorry. You just startled me. Are you okay?" He reached for her, then stopped himself. He'd almost pulled her against him to comfort her, to run his hands soothingly up her arms, and down her back.

He'd always been a physical person, given to casual hugs and comforting pats, but he realized she might not appreciate that sort of contact, especially after his initial attack. Besides, he was having a hard enough time thinking clearly without distracting himself further. Reining in his impulse to touch her, he hooked his thumbs safely into his jean pockets again and repeated, "Are you okay?"

"Yes, thank you." The hint of gratitude for his concern had lightened her eyes to a softer shade of green, but then she shifted her gaze quickly away from him, looking uncomfortable with the change in chemistry between them. "I, uh, was afraid the gator would go after you, too. I just wanted to warn you."

"Then I owe you my thanks *and* an apology." He extended his hand. "I'm Jack Forrester."

She didn't take his hand but slowly returned her gaze to his face. "I know who you are, Dr. Forrester."

He stared in surprise. Had he imagined the mocking emphasis on the word *doctor*, or the inexplicable gleam in those gray-green eyes? He certainly hadn't imagined her refusal of a courteous handshake. Withdrawing his hand, he said, "Then you have me at a disadvantage."

Her lips quirked to one side. Generous, shapely lips. Warmth again stirred low in his gut, even as a chord plucked in his memory. He'd seen those lips before, slanted in that exact same way, in a wry expression of annoyance. A nonverbal chiding for something stupid he'd said or done.

As he struggled to bring the memory into clear view, a blush crept into her face—a dusky-rose color that darkened the velvety skin just above and below her high cheekbones.

Recognition hit him, swift and hard. He felt as if a horse had kicked him in the stomach, or in the head. He almost saw stars. "Callie." Incredulity robbed him of all other words.

She simply arched a brow.

He drew in a slow, much-needed breath. *Callie Marshall.* She'd been his friend. His right-hand man. His best bud. He'd taught her how to gut a fish, how to throw a football, how to spit and hit her target. She'd taught him how to whistle between two fingers loud enough to hear at the other end of the Point.

Damn. Callie Marshall.

The skinny little tomboy who'd always worn her hair shorter than his and got her face dirtier than anybody's had blossomed into…by God…a woman.

And what a woman.

Now that he knew who she was, he could see that her eyes were basically the same. Maybe a little wider. Maybe a little greener. But why the *hell* hadn't he recognized them?

Or her mouth. It had been the sassiest mouth on the Point, spouting the most irreverent wisecracks a kid had ever gotten away with.

In their teenage years, he'd started noticing that mouth more and more, and not because of the things she said with it. Sometimes just a glance at Callie's smooth, full lips had made his insides warm up and his thoughts turn to kissing. It had embarrassed him, thinking that way about her. She'd looked more like a boy than a girl…except for her mouth.

The clue that had finally tipped him off today had been her blush. When most people blushed, their entire faces turned red. Not Callie's. Only her cheeks grew rosy, near her slanted cheekbones, as if an artist carefully brushed the color there whenever she got embarrassed, which she had every time he'd stared at her too long.

That discovery had also made him uncomfortable, back when he was sixteen, seventeen years old. He'd realized then that he'd better find a girlfriend. Someone he wouldn't mind getting worked up over.

He'd found one. A few, actually. But never another friend like Callie.

Gladness to see her swelled up in him, along with a

good measure of relief. No wonder he'd been so personally affected by the sight, the feel, the scent of her. On some subconscious level, he must have recognized her as one of his oldest, dearest friends.

That had to be it.

With a shake of his head, he laughed out loud. "Callie! Damn, it's good to see you. It's been too long. Way too long." He opened his arms to fold her into a welcoming hug.

She backed away, into the wall again. "No, wait."

He stopped, bewildered.

She gnawed on her bottom lip in clear dismay.

Concern and foreboding tempered his joy at seeing her. Something was wrong here. Definitely wrong. Although they'd never actually hugged as kids, they'd shared some fine times. Surely their reunion called for a friendly hug?

"I'm not here on a social visit, Jack. I mean—" she cleared her throat and straightened into a dignified pose "—Dr. Forrester."

His eyes narrowed. "Dr. Forrester?"

"I've got that right, don't I? I understand you're an orthopedic surgeon now, as well as a general practitioner." She smoothed her silky dark hair rather nervously, then brushed the sand off her blouse and skirt. "In case no one's pointed it out to you, that does entitle you to be called 'doctor.'"

"Ah. So that's why folks have been calling me that. I was beginning to wonder." He forced an amiable smile. "I'd say you know me well enough to call me Jack, wouldn't you?"

Something in her eyes flashed, like lightning on a stormy sea. His bewilderment deepened. What had he said that bothered her?

Her tone remained excruciatingly polite. "Thank

you, but I'd prefer to use your title. And you'll probably want to call me Ms. Marshall."

He frowned. She sounded as poised and impersonal
as a business-minded stranger. He couldn't let her get
away with that. Wedging a shoulder against the wall
and leaning deliberately closer than a stranger would
have dared, he asked in a soft, down-home drawl, "So,
what's going on, Cal?"

There went that blush again. And another mysterious flash in those eyes. But her chin came up and her
voice remained cool. "You remember Meg, don't you?
My sister?"

Of course he remembered Meg. His long-ago ro-
mance with her hadn't ended on a very good note.
There'd been quite a scene between them before he'd
left for college. Was Callie holding a grudge because of
his awkward breakup with her older sister all those
years ago? He found that hard to believe. He doubted
Meg herself would care much about it by now. Cautiously he replied, "Sure, I remember Meg."

"She's a lawyer."

"Is she? Good for her." He meant it. He'd always
liked Meg. "I figured she'd do well."

"And she's married. Her name's Crinshaw. Margaret Crinshaw."

After a moment's deliberation, Jack remembered
where he'd heard the name before, and felt his face
freeze into a bland mask. *Margaret Crinshaw. The attorney who was handling the malpractice suit against him.*

"I'm here on business, Dr. Forrester," Callie dis-
closed, her tone surprisingly gentle, "to investigate the
malpractice charge against you."

Slowly he straightened his stance. He couldn't find
the voice to reply. Callie Marshall had come back home
to build a case against him. She'd be working on Grant

Tierney's behalf—another weapon in his never-ending arsenal. Disappointment shot through Jack with stunning force. Anger, too. How could she side against him?

He was past the point of anger at Grant Tierney. He'd been his enemy for so long now, Jack expected the worst from him. The lawsuit itself wasn't particularly worrisome, either. He knew it held no merit. But Callie's cool announcement that she'd be working against him bothered the hell out of him.

Forcing his jaw to relax, he asked in a conversational tone, "Are you an attorney, too, then, *Ms. Marshall?*"

"No. An investigator." She strolled past him in her bare feet, across the tiled floor, looking tense but somehow regal. "I work for attorneys in Tallahassee. I help them gather facts and evidence for various cases."

"And this case is just…business as usual for you?"

"Yes." She avoided his gaze, training hers on the life jackets and rafts stacked against the far wall. "Business as usual. Meg felt I'd be the best investigator for this case since I'm familiar with the community."

"And why did Meg take the case?"

Callie lifted her shoulder in a dispassionate shrug. "She's known Grant as long as you have. She's been handling some of his real estate dealings, and saw no reason to turn down this case."

Jack inclined his head and studied her. Callie hadn't been the cool, detached kind when she was younger. She'd been passionate about every quest she'd ever undertaken, even if the goal was only to have a rollicking good time. She'd been passionate about her friendships, too, rushing to the aid of any pal in need. She'd been emotional. Reactive. Righteous. Open. Intensely loyal.

Now she claimed to be investigating this case

against him—her childhood friend—strictly for business reasons.

He didn't believe it. He'd seen the flash of emotion in her eyes, just moments ago. He wanted to know what that emotion had been, and why she was hiding it. Something had gone wrong—terribly wrong—for Callie Marshall to be working against him. Twelve years had passed and they'd lost touch, but she couldn't have changed that much.

"I'm not guilty of malpractice, Callie."

She held up a hand. "Stop right there. I can't discuss the case with you."

"You don't want to hear my side of it?"

"No." Her response had sounded too fervent, almost panicked, in the quiet of the boathouse. In a softer, more modulated tone, she amended, "At least, not now. I didn't come prepared to talk to you about it. I didn't even know this boathouse was yours. I was on my way to Grant Tierney's place. If it wasn't for that alligator, I'd—"

"When *will* you want to hear my side of the case?"

She eyed him in exasperation. "If I ever want to hear your side of it, Dr. Forrester, I'll ask for it."

He raised a brow. "Maybe I won't be willing to give it then."

She, too, raised a brow. "Maybe you won't have a choice."

A challenge, if he'd ever heard one.

The lady herself presented an even greater challenge. She intended to proceed with her "business as usual," as if their friendship had meant nothing to her. He knew her better than that, he swore he did. He just had to peel away this cool, polished coat of armor she was wearing and let the real Callie Marshall come out and play.

The evening suddenly held a lot of promise.

Crossing his arms, he shifted his weight into a confrontational wide-legged stance. "Are you telling me, Ms. Investigator, ma'am, that you just happened to be strolling by *my boathouse* when a gator showed up out of nowhere and, uh, chased you into it?"

Callie's eyes widened and her jaw lowered in indignation. "I didn't know it was your boathouse. It used to be Mr. Langley's. And no, I wasn't *strolling*. I was driving to Grant Tierney's beach house when my car got stuck in the sand. I had to—" She stopped herself, refusing to ramble on defensively. "Are you insinuating that I'm lying about the alligator for some underhanded purpose?"

"Now, now. I wouldn't use the term *lying*." He ambled toward a workbench and rested his hip against it. "Not in connection with a friend like you. I know you better than that."

She compressed her lips and felt her face warm. He'd made his point. Why should he believe her about the alligator when she refused to even listen to his side of the malpractice suit? She wouldn't be drawn into that game, though. He wouldn't use their previous relationship to manipulate her investigation. "The truth will eventually speak for itself. Sooner or later, you'll know there's an alligator outside, probably still lurking in those bushes."

"There haven't been many gators around these parts for years. Are you *sure* it was a gator?"

"Of course I'm sure." Did he really not believe her?

He frowned, plainly unconvinced. "What did he look like?"

"Well, he had short, stubby legs," she started, "and a long, ugly snout. And his skin was—oh, what do you mean, what did he look like? He looked like an alligator! And he was dragging something orange," she suddenly recalled. "Fabric, I think." Biting her lip with renewed anxiety, she wrapped her arms around herself, vaguely conscious of a pain near her ribs, just below her armpit. She'd taken a fall, she remembered. Ignoring the ache, she asked, "Do you think it could have been orange clothing? A T-shirt, maybe? Could he have attacked somebody?"

Jack squinted at her as if trying to decide how much stock to put in her story. "If it really is a gator, I suppose it's possible."

"It *is* a gator! You've got to believe me."

"There's one way to prove it beyond a doubt." He threw her a pointed glance. "I'm a great believer in proof, you know." His gaze then went to the door. With a decisive squaring of his jaw, he stalked toward it.

She lunged at his arm with a panicked cry, digging the fingers of both hands into his warm, muscled biceps and holding on until he stopped. "Don't you dare go out there! You could be killed."

"Oh, come on, Cal. Don't you think I could take on one measly little ol' gator?"

Fear nearly squeezed her breathless. She remembered the crazy, death-defying stunts he'd pulled as a kid—like diving from high, rocky waterfalls, leaping between speeding boats, or swimming in shark-infested waters. She'd tried a few crazy stunts herself. But she'd grown up. He obviously hadn't. Releasing his arm, she threw herself between him and the door. "You can't go out there."

His gaze played over her face, and familiar devils danced in his eyes. "That's not a dare, is it?"

"No!" she exclaimed with a gasp. "It's not!"

He grinned and reached around her for the door handle.

She shoved his arm away and jockeyed her position, shifting to block him. "This is serious, Jack. Alligators are man-eaters. They mutilate their prey, drown it and drag it to their lairs to rot. Do you want to rot, Jack? Do you?"

That gave him pause. He eased off in his attempt to reach the door handle and fixed her with a pondering look. "Doesn't sound too appealing," he mused. His face, she realized, was very near hers. He seemed to be giving the more gruesome aspects of gator behavior some serious thought.

She hoped he was. She truly hoped he was.

The moment stretched on, and she gradually became aware that she'd flattened her palms against his chest to hold him back. Smooth, hard muscle lay beneath the thin cotton of his T-shirt. She felt the strong, steady thumping of his heart, breathed in the virile warmth of his skin, thrilled to the power she sensed coiled within his lean body.

He'd grown so amazingly strong and muscular.

His salty, male scent provoked memories of times they'd wrestled around as kids. How different it would be to wrestle with him now. A slow, wicked heat spread through her at the thought. How very, very different.

"Maybe," he said in a solemn half-whisper, "I can outrun that gator, ma'am."

She blinked, stared, then snapped back to cold reality. "Outrun it!" she cried.

"My boat is only a few dozen yards away. A short stroll down the dock. Of course, I'd have to stop and unlock the door to the boat slip when I got there, but—"

"But nothing!" She shoved him as hard as she could, which barely set him back a step. He hadn't changed at all from the reckless daredevil he used to be. "You can't risk outrunning a gator. I'm lucky I made it in here alive. They're faster than horses. Like huge lizards. And you know how fast lizards can dart around."

"Darn fast," he agreed.

Was that amusement glinting in his eyes? "Damn you, Jack Forrester, do you believe me that there's a gator outside this door, or not?"

"Of course I do. You wouldn't be yelling, hanging on to me and clawing my chest if there wasn't. Unless, of course—" his voice dropped a husky decibel and his wide, firm mouth turned up at one end "—circumstances were very, very different."

His gaze meandered down her face in a thoroughly unsettling way. Warmth surged through her. She found it hard to breathe. He was teasing her, of course. Just teasing. But he'd never teased her in that particular way when they'd been kids. He'd never acknowledged that he was a man and she, a woman, or hinted at the things they could do.

"If you believe me about the alligator," she whispered, shaken beyond all reason, "then get serious about the danger we're facing. Don't scare me anymore."

"Just what is it you're scared of, Callie?"

Nothing scared her more than her heart-thudding response to his hoarse, intimate tone and searching stare. She found herself wanting to give him whatever he was looking for. And more.

"The alligator, of course," she managed to reply. Despite the chaotic pounding of her heart—and an increasing pain beneath her arm—she rallied enough to add, "I told you to call me Ms. Marshall."

He drew back slightly, his mouth a firm line. "In that case, Ms. Marshall, don't you worry. Gators are mean, but they can't break down doors." He nodded toward the door, then returned his gaze to hers. "As long as that one stays shut, we'll be safe and snug."

Safe and snug.

Stranded alone with him.

She considered outrunning that gator.

"Relax," Jack said, notably unperturbed. "We may be here awhile."

Her muscles tensed at the thought. She shouldn't be here, or anywhere near him. "How far away is your boat, did you say?"

"At least a hundred yards."

She frowned. Hadn't he said a few dozen before? "Isn't there any way to get to the boat from in here?"

"Nope. I added this storage room onto the back of the boathouse as an afterthought. We'd have to walk around the outside. And if we made it to the boat slip, we'd have to stop to unlock the door. Come to think of it... " He patted his pockets, as if searching for something, then grimaced. "I believe I dropped the key. I'll bet it's lying out there in the sand somewhere."

He shrugged apologetically. His windblown hair glimmered like a golden halo around his suntanned face. The angelic effect, however, only emphasized the rugged cut of his jaw, the savage scar on his cheek and the disturbing sparkle in his brown eyes.

Never had a man looked so much like an angel and a devil at the exact same time.

He reached behind her and flicked a switch. Light brightened the place. She glanced around and realized the room had been tiled and finished, complete with a sink, refrigerator and fish-cleaning board.

Before she could comment, Jack's gaze swung back to her in a double take and narrowed on her blouse, just beneath her left breast. "What's that?" He moved a step closer, scrutinizing. "Is that *blood?*"

She glanced down in surprise. She'd been conscious of pain since she'd fallen on the boathouse step, but hadn't thought much about it. Now she noticed a red stain slowly spreading across the white silk of her blouse.

Blood.

A feeling of wooziness came over her, and she looked away from the stain. She was an adult now. The sight of blood shouldn't bother her. Curling her bottom lip between her teeth, she forced the faintness away. The injury couldn't be too bad, she assured herself. It didn't hurt *that* much.

As the ramifications of her situation sank in, she devoutly hoped the bleeding would stop on its own *without* requiring the local doctor's attention.

Unfortunately, it seemed she already had his attention.

"What happened?" he demanded, drawing his golden-dark brows together in concern.

"I…I fell," she said, embarrassed to tell him even this much about the injury. "On the boathouse step, when I was running from the gator."

"I'd better take a look at it." Decisively he ordered, "Take off your blouse."

2

"Take off my blouse? Absolutely not. This little scratch doesn't need medical attention."

"And how do you know that?"

"It hardly hurts at all," Callie lied, trying to look unaffected by the pain even as she held her arm away from her body at an awkward angle. "What I really need is a cell phone. Don't you carry one for emergencies? We can call the authorities about the alligator. I tried my phone back at the car, but the batteries must have—"

"Sorry," Jack interrupted. "I'm not carrying a cell phone. They don't work well out here. I have a beeper, but that won't help us now. Besides, your injury might need stitches. Who else are you going to get on the Point to stitch you up?"

"I don't need stitches." She hoped. She didn't particularly like the idea of a needle piercing her flesh. Even worse, though, was the prospect of taking her blouse off in front of him.

He frowned. "You're not afraid to let me take a look at your wound because of that lawsuit, are you?" He peered suspiciously at her. "You're not doubting my intentions, or my ability to help?"

"I hadn't thought of that," she admitted with surprise. She had every right to worry about a doctor she was investigating for malpractice. She didn't doubt his

intentions were good, though, or that he was capable
of dressing a wound.

"The claim is bogus, Callie. Malicious."

She pursed her mouth. She wasn't in the best position to challenge that. Not while she was stranded
alone with him and struggling to ignore the sweet me-
tallic scent of blood and the slippery feel of it against
her skin. "We'll see."

"Yes, we will. If you don't bleed to death first."

She felt herself blanch. Surely the bleeding would
stop soon. Surely they'd think of a way out of here. "It
barely hurts," she maintained, feeling light-headed.
"It's nothing."

Jack raised a shoulder. "Then please, make yourself
at home." He gestured toward a few patio chairs.
"Have a seat. Feel free to bleed as much as you'd like.
Ooze to your heart's content."

She lifted her chin at his sarcasm. That small act of
defiance made her dizzy.

With a rueful smirk, he muttered, "I'll round up
some first-aid supplies. Get that damp, sandy blouse
off the wound, and sit down before you fall down."

Callie swallowed against a suddenly dry throat and
sat down in a patio chair, while Jack strode to a stain-
less steel sink and rifled through an upper cabinet. His
muscle-hugging shirt and tight jeans drew her gaze to
places she shouldn't be noticing. He looked strikingly
unlike any doctor she'd ever visited.

*But he is a doctor. He sees women without their blouses
every day.* No amount of reasoning helped. She
couldn't, wouldn't, take her blouse off in front of him.

The pain in her ribs—below her armpit, near her
breast—began to seriously throb. What damage had
she done? She lifted her arm and craned her neck to
see, but her breast got in the way. Unwilling to let this

inconvenience dissuade her, she said, "If you'll just lend me a wet cloth, a bandage and some ointment, I can patch this up myself."

"Yeah, you're a real Florence Nightingale." He shot her a droll glance. "Don't look at it, Cal. If you pass out, you'll hurt yourself even worse."

Feeling undeniably woozy, she focused on him instead of her wound. He retrieved a large white box from the upper shelf, then turned on the water and thoroughly soaped his hands clear up to his wrists, as if he were scrubbing for surgery.

Anxiety knotted her stomach. "Give me a little more credit than that," she chided with false bravado. "I haven't passed out over the sight of blood in years. I'm not a kid anymore, in case you haven't noticed."

He paused. Smoothly, then, he dried his hands, ambled toward her with the medical kit and pulled up a chair. Leaning close, he met her gaze. "I've noticed."

An illogical warmth flushed through her.

She could see how her sister had fallen in love with him. His potent masculinity and dark, stirring regard were enough to disarm any woman. Except her. She knew him too well to allow her common sense to melt away in the heat of his stare.

"Your blouse is still on."

She felt a flush climb into her cheeks. "Even if you treat this wound for me, I'm still investigating the case against you. Just because you're being nice doesn't mean—"

"So that's the problem. You think you'll be indebted. Forget it. I'm only doing what has to be done. I mean, how would it look in the headlines—Woman Bleeds to Death in Surgeon's Boathouse." He shook his head in mock reflection. "Couldn't be good for business."

She almost gave in to a smile. Almost.

Her anxiety wouldn't allow it. Her hands involuntarily clutched the fabric below her collar, closing defensively over the top buttons. "Jack," she whispered, her back against the proverbial wall, "I...I can't take my blouse off in front of you."

He stared at her, incredulous. "You're embarrassed to take off your blouse?"

She nodded.

"Do you want me to turn around while you take it off?"

"What good would that do? I'd still be sitting here in my...my..." Her voice faded into tense, uncomfortable silence.

Their gazes shifted and danced. Hers asked for understanding. His refused to give it.

The deed had to be done.

"Close your eyes, Callie." He said it quietly but with the same sternness he had used when he'd taken bee stingers out of her foot or slivers out of her fingers.

She understood that his words, though sternly spoken, were more of an offer than an order. They meant that she could close her eyes, divorce herself from whatever unpleasantness had to be faced, and he would handle it for her. He would make everything okay.

Maybe because he always had, Callie closed her eyes. She couldn't, however, distance herself quite as easily as she had when they'd been kids. She braced herself—not only for the physical pain, but for the abject humiliation.

He loosened her grip on the front of her blouse, gently prying open her fingers, and set her hands on the arms of the chair. Then he began unbuttoning.

She kept her eyes tightly shut. She couldn't believe this was happening. *Jack Forrester was unbuttoning her blouse.* The top button. The second. The third. Her heart beat wildly. He was going to take the blouse off her. She'd be sitting here in her semi-sheer white bra.

From an influx of relative coolness, she knew he'd finished and had opened the blouse. If any part of her body other than her cheeks could blush, she'd be redder than a lobster.

"Have you heard about Earline?" he asked in an absent tone.

"Earline?" she repeated through stiff lips. He was drawing the silk down the shoulder of her uninjured side. Which meant, of course, that her bra was exposed to his view. A warm shiver raced across her suddenly sensitized skin.

"Earline's the best thing that's happened to me in years. She's a real beauty. I've been the envy of every guy on the Point. You'll have to drop by my house and meet her sometime."

"Your girlfriend lives with you?" Callie didn't know why that surprised her. Jack Forrester exuded sensuality like most people did body heat. Why wouldn't he have a live-in girlfriend? And why should that prospect settle in her stomach like an undigested lump?

"She's not my girlfriend." He guided her arm out of the blouse, his fingers strong, warm and controlling. "My relationship with Earline is a lot more official than that. A matter of public record."

Public record? That could only mean...

"She's your *wife?*" The idea stunned her. An invisible cord seemed to wrap painfully around her internal organs. She opened one eye to read his face. "You're married?"

"Nah. You know me better than that." He tossed her blouse aside, held her arm up and bent his shaggy blond head closer to the underside of her left breast.

The stubble on his jaw glinted golden below the jagged scar on his cheek.

"Then what the hell are you talking about, 'matter of public record'?" She opened both eyes in bewilderment and, undeniably, relief. He wasn't married. Why should she care? She didn't! "Who's Earline?"

He answered with a roguish smile. "She's the sweetest, prettiest—" he paused to press something cold and wet against her injured skin, which made her jump "—mackerel that's ever been caught off the Point."

"Mackerel? Did you say, *mackerel?*"

"The biggest one caught around here in years. The record is posted at the marina, officially signed and notarized by all the proper authorities."

If he hadn't been holding her arm up and swabbing disinfectant on an area of skin that hurt so badly, Callie would have slugged him. "I figured you'd take the news about Earline hard," he murmured, his brown eyes sparkling with fun.

It was then that the significance of Earline hit home. "Are you telling me that your Earline is bigger than my Earl?"

"By a pound and a half."

"I don't believe it." She'd been so proud of holding that particular record. She still felt rather proud, and ridiculously pleased that he'd named his catch Earline. A fitting tribute to *her* long-ago catch. "Were you the first to break my record in twelve years?"

"Kermit Jones broke it five years ago, but only by half a pound. Take a deep breath now, Cal. You'll feel some pressure while I apply this bandage."

The pain caused her to wince, but not enough to distract her from the point she intended to make. "You realize you'll have to hold your record for seven long years to really beat me."

"No, darlin'." He sat up to confront her, angled his ruggedly handsome face and locked her in his shining gaze. "You'll have to catch a bigger mackerel to beat *me.*"

Neither of them actually smiled.

Neither of them looked away.

And there was no reason—none at all—for the joyful languor that warmed her insides and filled her head with thoughts of kissing him. There was no reason, either, for his gaze to sweep slowly across her mouth.

Sensuality skittered through her veins.

It meant nothing, she told herself. She'd misinterpreted his gazes before. He'd looked at her that way a couple of times when they'd been teenagers, only to break the moment with a silly wisecrack and busy himself with other friends. Girlfriends, usually. Which had been fine with her.

"Are we almost finished here, Doc?" She broke the moment herself this time.

His eyes flickered back to hers with a dazed expression. After a moment, he breathed in deeply through his nostrils and blew the breath back out. "Uh, no."

She raised an inquiring brow.

"The part of the wound I've dressed so far," he explained, "is only a scrape. I haven't been able to see the rest."

Foreboding gathered in her stomach. "Why not?"

"It's beneath the side band of your bra."

"My bra?" she breathed.

"It'll have to come off, Callie." He said it as if he were breaking news of a necessary amputation.

She stared at him, aghast. He expected her to take off her *bra?*

"It looks like a fairly deep gash," he told her. "The tightness of the band may be acting as a bandage and inhibiting some serious bleeding. I have to take a closer look."

"C-can't we just loosen the straps?" she stuttered, her hands crossing to cover her lace-clad breasts. "You know, loosen them just enough so you can—"

"The bra has to come off," he stated. "Even after I've treated the wound, you can't wear anything too binding over it." Her heart tripped into a faster, heavier beat. Heat crept under her skin. Her nipples tightened into sensitive buds at the thought of baring her breasts for him. "No."

He sat back and crossed his muscular arms. "You haven't been too embarrassed so far," he reasoned, "have you?"

She admitted to herself that he was right. She'd been sitting here in her semisheer bra without much embarrassment at all. He'd distracted her, of course.

But he also hadn't given her breasts a glance. Not even one covert peek, as far as she could tell. He seemed unaffected by her partial nakedness. For all the interest he'd shown, she could still be a gawky, flat-chested kid with braces.

The thought irked her. She might not have blossomed into a raving beauty, and might not be exactly stacked, but her breasts had grown considerably since she'd left. Considerably! She'd actually made it to a B cup.

"I know this is a cliché," he said, sitting forward, "but there's nothing you've got that I haven't seen before."

That set her teeth lightly on edge. It *was* a cliché. It was also the truth. That didn't make the statement any less troubling. He was, in effect, telling her that she had nothing that could interest him.

The more she thought about it, the more it sounded like a challenge.

"Close your eyes again, Callie."

"No," she softly replied, unable to stop from acting on an impulse. "I think I'd rather keep them open this time."

He studied her face in patent surprise, as if trying to divine her meaning. "Actually, I'd prefer that you close them," he countered. "Until I get the bandage in place, there might be some...unpleasantness."

"I'm a big girl now," she drawled in a whisper. She touched a fingertip to each satiny bra strap on her shoulders, then slowly drew those fingertips down to the lace-trimmed cups. "I can take it, Doc."

His eyes followed the path of her fingers.

With her heart thudding, she skimmed her fingers along the top edges of her bra, around the gentle swells of her cleavage, until she reached the front clasp. "Should *I* take it off, or—" she inclined her head and stared at him "—should *you?*"

His mouth opened an instant before the gruff words came out. "Whichever you'd prefer."

She focused on his dark, unreadable face. He focused on the clasp, which she gripped with trembling fingers. He sat perfectly still, his face void of reaction, and watched her fingers work.

The hook gave way. Self-conscious heat rose up her neck and flooded her face. She opened the bra. Parted it. Her breasts sprang free of the lace.

He moved not a muscle. His gaze didn't shift to either side, but remained fixed in place, straight ahead, as if he'd slipped into a daydream. He looked utterly oblivious.

Her heart gave a bleak little pang. It was true, then. He had no more interest in her now than he ever had. "I may need your help taking this off the rest of the way," she said, humiliated by her own bold behavior and by her genuine need for his help. The loosening of the bra had renewed the throbbing in the wound. Her pride, however, throbbed even more. Amazing, how much bruised pride could hurt. "I'm afraid of disrupting the injury."

Slowly, as if he'd just then realized she was still there, his gaze inched upward. And locked with hers.

The heated intensity of his stare shocked her.

"Callie," he rasped. "Take my shirt."

Before she understood, he'd pulled his T-shirt up and over his head. His magnificent chest rippled with muscle beneath a gilded spangling of curls as he handed the T-shirt to her.

"Use it as a drape," he gruffly ordered. When she hesitated, unsure of what he meant, he took the body-warmed shirt from her, draped it over her shoulder and fanned its cottony folds across her breasts, taking care not to touch her.

"We might get blood on it." She barely recognized the husky whisper as her own. His unexpected reaction had shaken the breath out of her, and the sight of him shirtless—golden, muscled and hairy—kept her spellbound.

"That's okay. I don't mind a little blood."

The impulse seized her to run her hands over every sleekly muscled contour, tangle her fingers in his silky curls, trace the light, jagged slash of a scar above his left nipple. "Take your shirt back," she urged. "I don't care if I have a cover."

His stare shot back to hers, stunning her again with its raw intensity. "I do."

The blaze in his eyes ignited little fires in her blood. Thrilling her. Scaring her. She'd never seen him like this before. She wanted to back away. She wanted to move closer.

He wrenched his gaze from her and returned to his task. Thick, heated silence descended between them, broken only by the murmur of the surf, the sigh of summer breezes through the boathouse and the occasional cry of a gull.

Jack heard nothing but the blood drumming in his ears as he drew the straps of the opened bra from her silky shoulders and carefully removed the side band from her wound.

He would concentrate only on his work.

Gritting his teeth seemed to help a little. Nothing helped much, though. Why the hell had he thought he could watch Callie unveil her breasts and keep himself under control? He'd had a hard enough time unbuttoning her blouse and avoiding the sight of her pert, dark-tipped breasts beneath white lace.

He didn't understand his intensely physical reaction to her. It wasn't as if he'd never seen breasts before.

And yet, it was. *As if he'd never seen breasts before.*

Cursing himself and his unwanted arousal, he worked quickly. Silently. He had to forget this was Callie's skin he was touching. Callie's scent he was breathing. Callie's breasts barely covered, close enough that he could turn his head and brush his face against them. Take the dusky, pointed nipples into his mouth.

Sexual heat washed through him. He had to think of another topic. He'd latched onto his earlier conversation about Earline like a drowning man grabbing for a lifeboat. Distracting himself hadn't been easy.

He'd never had a problem keeping his mind on the

job before. Of the many women he'd seen in the course of his work, no one had rattled him, tempted him or made him ache with desire. No one except Callie.

Maybe because of his history with her. When he'd been a randy teenager, he'd caught glimpses of her small breasts through certain shirts and swimsuits. Her flowerlike nipples had somewhat obsessed him, turning from blossom soft to pebble hard in the space of a missed heartbeat. All it took was a splash of cool water or a chilly breeze. Or, sometimes, a simple stare.

He'd never deliberately stared at her. He hadn't felt right, thinking about her in a sexual way. He'd spent whole nights trying not to think about naive, wide-eyed Callie and her pebble-tipped breasts.

He tried not to think about them now. But the drape had slipped a little, and the lush, pale side-swell of her breast loomed near his fingers. The temptation to nudge his knuckles into the silky softness sent a shaft of heat through his loins.

He gritted his teeth harder and finished the bandaging job.

With acute relief that the work was done, he raised his head to inform her she didn't need stitches. His eyes met hers, and his words dissolved in another onslaught of heat.

This one came from the way she was looking at him. In place of wide-eyed naiveté was a subtle, smoky awareness. Sensual awareness. She knew that he wanted her. And she wasn't displeased with that knowledge.

"All finished, Doc?" The huskiness of her voice reminded him of the way she'd spoken, the way she'd watched him, as she'd unclasped her bra. He'd been too caught up in the moment to notice then.

Was she teasing him? Or, inviting him?

"The bandages are in place," he slowly replied, unable to look away from her sultry green gaze or to forget that they sat half-naked, both of them, and within easy reaching distance. "You won't need stitches."

She didn't answer. She merely sat with his T-shirt draped across her peaking breasts, her shoulders and arms sleek and bare, her lips peachy smooth, her eyes sensually dazed.

Her stare slowly descended to his mouth.

Desire to kiss her ripped through him. To kiss her. Feel her. Taste her. Every muscle in his body clenched with need.

Did she know what she was doing to him? Did she know he couldn't, as a doctor treating her wound, act on his desire?

A clear invitation, however, might allow him to shift out of doctor mode, now that the treatment had ended.

"Don't play with fire, Callie," he warned in a low, hoarse whisper, aware he was treading a fine ethical line, "unless you want to get hot."

Her gaze focused on his.

"If that's what you want, though." He angled his face near hers. "Let's strike the match."

A strangled sound rose from her throat, and she pulled back from him. "What are you talking about?" The shirt fell from her shoulder, and she caught it against her chest with both hands, looking thoroughly flustered.

Disappointment clutched him. Could he have been wrong? Could his own crazy desire have made him imagine her provocative air? "I think you know."

As if sensing his uncertainty, she gathered her poise and glared at him. "What exactly are you trying to say, *Doctor?*"

That was when he knew, beyond a doubt, she'd been teasing him. Ms. Callie Marshall might not be ready to kiss him, but she wasn't above playing games. From the time she'd been a kid, she'd reacted with the same red-faced indignation whenever she'd had to bluff her way out of a tight spot.

He wasn't sure if he wanted to laugh or to shake her. Mostly he wanted to kiss her. "Get dressed, before I ask for my T-shirt back."

He had the satisfaction of seeing worry flash in those gray-green eyes, just before he turned his back on her. Too bad he didn't have a shower handy—a nice, ice-cold shower. He sorely needed one.

As he washed his hands at the sink, she called, "Is it okay if I wear your shirt for now?" Her voice had lost its indignation. She'd adopted a notably humble tone. "My blouse is a mess, and, uh, without my bra, it would be too sheer to wear."

The image conjured up by those words only aggravated his condition. "By all means, wear the T-shirt. *Please.*"

Callie bit her lip, feeling guilty. He'd treated her injury in a kind, professional manner, and what had she done? She'd pushed him into noticing her as a woman. Flaunted herself.

And boy, had it worked.

Heat flushed through her at the memory, and not all because of embarrassment. He'd reacted so intensely. What would he have done if she hadn't pulled away? Her pulse rioted at the possibilities.

Turning her back to him, she slipped his T-shirt over her head and pulled it down over her naked breasts, conscious of the pain in her side. The injury felt much better than it had, though, now that it was clean, dry and securely bandaged.

She really did owe him her thanks.

"Jack." Nervously she turned to face him. "I want to thank you for your help."

"You're welcome." He didn't spare her a glance but sauntered toward the refrigerator, looking gloriously male in his tight, faded jeans, his golden-furred chest with its mysterious scar, and sinewy biceps browned to a shimmery tan. "Want a beer?"

"A beer? Oh…no. No thanks. It's getting pretty late." She glanced at the twilight colors blazing outside the high, dusty windows. "We need to figure out a way to reach the authorities before that alligator hurts someone."

He grabbed a bottle of beer and popped the cap off with his thumb. "I could wire up my old ship-to-shore radio." He nodded toward a dusty case on the shelf. "I haven't used it in years, though. Parts may be missing."

"It's worth a try." She gnawed at her bottom lip. "But what if it doesn't work?"

A slow, crooked smile spread across his mouth and somehow made her heart beat faster. "Then I guess we'll have to wait until someone rescues us."

"But that could take hours." She wasn't supposed to be with him at all. People could get the wrong idea. They might think she was fraternizing with him. Her sister's case could be compromised.

"Don't you worry." He sank his lean, muscled body into a chair and extended his long legs out in front of him. "If worse comes to worst, I can inflate a lifeboat, fill it with life jackets and make us a fairly cozy bed."

"Bed?" She gaped at him. "Why would we need a bed? You can't mean—" Horror momentarily robbed her of speech. "You don't think we'll have to stay here all night, do you?"

He took a swig of beer. "Look on the bright side. As

my father used to say, 'For every dark horizon, there's a sun waiting to rise.' We've got a refrigerator full of drinks, a cupboard of canned goods, and fine company." He lifted the beer to her in an amiable salute.

"But I...I have to get to a phone. I've got people to call, places to go. Things to do. I can't possibly stay here."

He pondered that for a moment. "I'd offer again to outrun the gator, but it's almost dark now." He leaned forward in his chair, holding the beer loosely between his outspread knees, and warned in an ominous tone, "It's a well-known fact that gators go into a feeding frenzy just before dark."

Callie swallowed a cry of dismay and dug her nails into her palms. She was beginning to feel truly trapped. "Let's try to wire that radio."

"We can try," he said with a pessimistic tilt of his head, "but—"

A sudden rapping at the door startled them both.

They glanced at each other in surprise, then moved toward the door in unison. "Who the hell...?" Jack muttered.

"Thank God," Callie cried. In the next heartbeat, though, she gasped. "The alligator! It could attack whoever's there."

Jack pushed the door open, looking more displeased than worried. Callie hovered at his elbow, torn between relief at being rescued and dread of a possible gator attack.

"Sheriff Gallagher," Jack greeted, not exactly in welcome.

"Howdy, Doc," wheezed the squat, balding lawman with a ruddy face. "We got a phone call from someone stuck on Gulf Beach Road. My clerk couldn't make out much of what the lady said before the connection went dead, but I—''

"I made the call, Sheriff." Callie shouldered her way past Jack and grabbed hold of the lawman's hefty arm, her gaze riveted on the bushes beyond. "Come in, come in, quick!" His squinty eyes rounded as she yanked him into the boathouse and slammed the door. "Do you have a cell phone with you, or a radio? Oh, I see you have a gun. I hope we won't need to use that, but if worse comes to worst—''

"Pardon me, please, ma'am," the sheriff interrupted, blinking at her in bewilderment, "but you seem mighty shaken up over something, talking about guns and all. What's the problem?"

"Uh, Sheriff Gallagher, this is Callie Marshall," Jack interrupted. "You remember her, don't you? Colonel Marshall's youngest girl?"

"Callie Marshall. Well, I'll be!" Wreaths of smiles crinkled his round face. "Haven't you grown into quite the lady! Never would have thunk it, back then. Your daddy would be proud enough to bust a gut if he could see you now."

The usual mix of grief and regret lanced through her at the mention of her father. At one time, she would have given anything to make him proud. But then she'd realized the futility of that yearning. She'd have to be one of his soldiers to earn his approval—one of his best soldiers. A mere daughter could never measure up. "Thank you."

"I was sorry to hear about his passing away. He was my poker-playing buddy, you know, whenever he stayed on the Point. I heard he died during a military expedition overseas."

"Yes." She'd heard that, too—many months after the fact. It had taken the authorities that long to contact her. His colleagues hadn't been aware he'd had any family left, after his wife had died. They'd been more right than they knew.

"My sympathies to you and your sister."

Callie simply stared, unable to respond. She felt as if an old wound had been torn open. She'd known it would be hard, coming back here.

"It's nice to see you've finally made it home for a visit."

Gathering her poise around her like a shield, she turned her thoughts away from hurtful topics. "Actually, Sheriff, I'm here on business. Now, as I was saying, there's an—"

"Meg's a lawyer now, Sheriff," Jack said. "A big-time lawyer in Tallahassee."

"Is she, by God? Always thought she was more the debutante type."

"Sheriff, please!" Callie burst out. "We have a potential crisis on our hands." The sheriff blinked another couple times. Callie pointed dramatically toward the door. "There's an alligator out there, and he's acting hungry. He chased me."

"An alligator?" The sheriff turned a questioning frown to Jack, who, curiously enough, responded with a wince.

Callie couldn't believe that Jack wasn't backing her up. "I swear it's true, Sheriff. Maybe Dr. Forrester doesn't entirely believe me, but a gator chased me down the beach. I've been so worried that he'll attack someone."

"Heck," said the sheriff, "you prob'ly saw old Alfred."

"Old Alfred?" Callie frowned. The sheriff obviously hadn't understood.

"Alfred is the only gator we have left on the Point, ma'am. He won't hurt nobody."

Callie stared at him blankly.

"A family who used to live down the beach started feeding him about ten years ago. Made him into a pet. When they moved away, he sallied over to Doc's property. I doubt if old Alfred remembers much about hunting for food. He'd prob'ly starve to death. Doc takes real good care of Alfred, though."

Callie turned her stunned gaze to Jack. "Alfred?"

Jack didn't seem to be following the conversation. He'd hooked his thumbs into his jeans pockets, pursed his lips and was studying the ceiling.

"Doc even tied an orange tag around him to make sure our local folks don't accidentally trap him," Sheriff Gallagher related, his voice warm with fatherly approval.

Callie felt her insides clenching and her temperature rising. "Dr. Forrester," she said in a deadly quiet voice, "do you have an alligator on the premises named Alfred?"

Jack cleared his throat, rubbed the back of his neck and awkwardly jerked his gaze back to her. "Come to think of it, Alfred might be somewhere in the vicinity."

Slow, hot anger flared red before her eyes. "And you let me go on thinking we were in danger?"

He cleared his throat again. "How could I be sure that a strange gator hadn't migrated to the Point?"

"Dressed in orange?" she fumed.

Sheriff Gallagher blinked in confusion, shifting his concerned gaze between them. "Calm down, now, Miss Callie." He patted her arm. "Doc prob'ly forgot about old Alfred."

"Forgot!" Callie shook the sheriff's hand off her arm

and glared at Jack. "I barricaded the door with my body to stop you from risking your life!"

"Told you I could take on that measly old gator."

She ground her teeth in rage. "What right do you have letting an alligator loose?"

"I didn't let him loose. He's in his natural habitat. And he's harmless. Old. Almost toothless."

"Toothless?" She crossed her arms and softened her voice to a purr. "Does he go into a feeding frenzy just before dark?"

Jack had the grace to flush beneath his tan, although a grin tugged at the corner of his mouth. "No, but I have caught him a time or two dragging his meat back to his lair to rot."

Her eyes widened in mute fury.

"Prob'ly easier for him to chew that way," theorized the sheriff. "Never knew old Alfred was toothless."

Callie balled her hands into fists, mostly to keep from strangling Jack. "You were going to keep me here until morning, weren't you?"

"No, no. Well, maybe. But—"

"You are despicable!" The words, of course, didn't do anywhere near the damage she wanted to inflict. "The sight of that gator is enough to give someone a heart attack," she raged. "Then the poor sap would have to travel fifty miles to find competent medical help."

The humor vanished from his eyes. "That's a hell of a thing to say, Callie."

"But true. And don't ever call me Callie again. It's Ms. Marshall to you, you…you…liar!" She barged past the sheriff and slung open the door.

"Damn it, Callie, wait just a minute," Jack called as she flew down the steps. "I didn't lie. Not really. In fact, I told you there weren't many gators left on the Point."

"Go to hell, Jack Forrester," she called over her shoulder. "And don't come near me again, or I'll have a peace warrant sworn out against you."

"Hey, *you* were the one who came onto *my* property. We both know you bodily threw yourself at me."

Her jaw dropped, and she whirled around to stare death rays through him. She couldn't even bring herself to reply, she was so angry.

"Um, excuse me, Miss Callie." The sheriff scuttled down the steps toward her. "It's getting dark, and I saw your car stuck in the marsh. I'd be honored to drive you somewhere."

Through the red haze of her fury, she realized that it was indeed getting dark, and she still had quite a walk to Grant Tierney's beach house. She couldn't very well drop in on him this late, anyway, especially wearing a man's T-shirt over her skirt and looking a complete mess. "Thank you, Sheriff," she replied, striving to unclench her jaw and strike a courteous tone. "I would indeed appreciate it, sir, if you could get me the hell out of here."

From the top of the boathouse steps, Jack called, "Callie..."

"Don't!" She brandished an index finger at him as if it were a gun. "You go ahead and enjoy your chuckle tonight, Dr. Forrester. But remember..." Her words dripped deadly acid. "For every bright horizon, there's a sun just waiting to sink. See you in court."

She marched righteously toward the sheriff's patrol car.

Flexing his lips into a tight, grim line, Jack Forrester watched her leave. "No, ma'am," he murmured to himself. "You'll see me way before that."

3

THE MAN WAS a danger.

After a long evening of mentally ranting at him and herself in her suite at the Bayside Bed-'n-Breakfast Inn, Callie had lapsed into a stirringly sensual dream about Jack Forrester with his heated stare and his tightly muscled body, making slow, hard love to her against the boathouse wall.

She awoke in a sweat.

No doubt about it, the man was a danger. He'd made a fool of her, threatened her credibility as an investigator for this case and, worst of all, stirred up dangerous physical longings. She couldn't afford that kind of vulnerability.

Jack Forrester wasn't to be trusted.

She would never forget the first time she'd learned that lesson. She'd just turned seventeen. Meg, two years her senior, had been slipping out at night with Jack, the love of her young life—a hell-raising nineteen-year-old with a budding reputation for fast cars, boats, motorcycles and women.

Meg hid the relationship from her father.

The Colonel had never approved of his daughters' dating, let alone dating wild Jack Forrester. The Colonel's temper, always bad, had grown worse over the years since their mother had died. Without her softening influence, he treated them more like soldiers than daughters, demanding absolute control over every aspect of their lives: no boys, no cars, no parties. No friends at the house. No pets. Straight A's in school, a ten-o'clock curfew, endless chores, grueling inspections, impossible standards.

They couldn't help leading secret lives, whenever and however they could.

When the Colonel learned from a friend that Meg was secretly dating Jack, he exploded into a fearsome rage. For the first time in her life, Meg refused to back down. She badly needed her freedom. Callie staunchly supported her. The Colonel viewed their united stand as an insurrection. He gave them an ultimatum: obey, or leave and never come back.

Callie couldn't believe he meant it. It seemed a terrible betrayal. She had to test him, had to know if he loved her, or if he truly wanted her out of his life.

She and Meg chose to leave.

"Jack has a car and money," Meg had said. "He can take us away from here." She called him, but he wasn't home. They packed their bags, crept from the house in the dead of night and set out to find Jack. They both knew they could count on him. He'd been Callie's pal her entire life, and he'd dated Meg most of the summer.

They found him at a beach bonfire party, cuddling with another girl. Callie still winced at the humiliating memory of the scene Meg had caused. Jack left the party with her, but only to end their relationship. "I'm not ready to get serious about anyone, Meg. If you are, find someone else."

Meg had been too hurt and angry to inform him of their plans, but Callie told him about the Colonel's ultimatum.

"You're just a kid, Cal. You can't make it on your own. Go home. Both of you."

Callie told him to go to hell. Meg seconded that idea. They hitchhiked to Tallahassee, pawned the jewelry their mother had left them and found jobs as waitresses. Life was tough—incredibly tough—but by pooling their resources, they survived.

They heard from friends that the Colonel spent little time at his house on Moccasin Point. It seemed he'd become more actively involved in overseas assignments.

And Jack had gone off to college.

Meg eventually married a wonderful guy who put her through college and law school. With her help, Callie started the investigative business and built it into a lucrative concern.

But the memory of their struggle, the Colonel's ultimatum and Jack's betrayal remained like a painful burr in Callie's heart. The two men she'd loved the most in the world had turned their backs on her when she'd needed them most.

She'd spent the next twelve years concentrating on her career, making sure she'd never need anyone that badly again.

Not for the first time, she wondered if vengeance against Jack had played any part in Meg's acceptance of this case. Meg had denied it. "I barely remember Jack Forrester. Grant Tierney, on the other hand, is a regular client of mine. Why shouldn't I take this case on behalf of his mother?"

"Can you honestly say that your past relationship with Jack won't affect your judgment?"

"For heaven's sake, Callie, I'm a happily married woman and the mother of two. I haven't given Jack Forrester a thought in years. But if his negligence really did cause Agnes Tierney's pain and suffering, I intend to make him pay."

"And if he wasn't negligent?"

Meg had hesitated for only a moment. "That's why I'm hiring you. I want you to dig out the facts. Our case has to be airtight. If we win, Grant Tierney will channel his corporate business through me. He could be my ticket into a partnership."

Callie still had her doubts about the wisdom of accepting the case, but her sister was, after all, the attorney. Callie depended on her law firm for a good deal of her investigative work. If Meg insisted on taking the case, Callie wanted her to go into that courtroom armed with facts and hard evidence.

With a renewed sense of mission, Callie climbed the stairway to Grant and Agnes Tierney's impressive gray brick home built on pilings. How glad she was that she hadn't been forced to trudge up to this stately door in her bedraggled condition yesterday. Dressed now in an immaculate beige linen suit, a cream silk shell and leather pumps, Callie rang the doorbell.

"Callie Marshall. Hello."

She recognized the tall, dark-haired man with winged brows, crystal-blue eyes and a charmingly dimpled smile more from recent visits to Meg's office than from childhood. A little older than Meg and her, Grant Tierney hadn't associated with them much as a kid. He'd spent most of his time away at exclusive schools, residing on the Point only during summer vacations.

Jack, who lived next door to the Tierneys, had known Grant better than any of the other Moccasin Point kids had. He'd considered Grant a friend. Had the friendship soured before the alleged malpractice, or because of it?

With a firm handshake, Callie apologized as she had yesterday for postponing their meeting.

"Don't give it another thought," Grant said in a pleasantly cultured voice that conveyed his moneyed upbringing. "I should have warned you not to take Gulf Beach Road. It's been closed for years. The sign must have fallen down. Thank heaven, Sheriff Gallagher found you."

Callie nodded in agreement and changed the subject by admiring the opulent decor of the spacious living room with its paintings, sculptures and potted plants. She had no desire to discuss yesterday's misadventures. She hadn't mentioned where the sheriff had found her or with whom. She'd be more prepared to explain those embarrassing details later, if necessary. She hoped it would never be necessary.

"You remember my mother, don't you?" Grant said.

Callie turned to Agnes Tierney with a fond smile. She remembered peering over the fence surrounding the Tierneys' garden to catch glimpses of the willowy, dreamy-eyed sculptress at work. Her hair was still a bright red and her eyes a striking sky blue. Dressed in a long, gauzy purple garment with wide, flowing sleeves, Agnes looked like some exotic, colorful bird.

Clasping her graceful, age-spotted hands together, she cried, "Isn't it absolutely *perfect*?"

Callie hesitated, unsure of how to answer the vague but enthusiastic question.

Agnes thrust her face closer to Callie's. "Oh, Grant, it *is* perfect. This nose. This fabulous nose. I must capture it!"

"Uh, Mother." Grant cast an apologetic smile to Callie, who resisted the impulse to shield her nose with her hands. "I believe you're alarming our guest."

Agnes reluctantly drew back. "Did I alarm you? I'm sorry. But your nose would be perfect for my Venus."

"Aren't you forgetting something, Mother?"

Agnes raised her lightly penciled mauve brows. Grant reached out and tapped her right hand. Her gaze went to that hand, and her joy extinguished like a snuffed-out candle. "Oh, that's right. I can't finish my Venus, can I?"

"I'm afraid not," her son gently replied. To Callie, he explained, "She's lost dexterity in her sculpting hand."

The pained look of resignation on Agnes's face touched Callie with sympathy. "I'd like to ask you some questions about your injury, Mrs. Tierney."

"Come, have a seat, and we'll get down to work." Grant ushered his mother and Callie to armchairs shaped like cupped hands near a coffee table of glossy petrified wood. "It's taking Mother a while to adjust. The handicap has been an emotional drain, and a financial one. She has contracts to sculpt busts of a dozen celebrities, but won't be able to do any of them now."

Callie took a cassette recorder from her purse. "Mrs. Tierney, I'd like you to tell me what happened. Do you mind if I record our conversation?"

Agnes consented to the recording, then began, "We were at the Fourth of July picnic, and I was having a wonderful chat with nice Mr. Sullivan, a very handsome man. A Libra, like me. He has the loveliest home on the Point. Anyway, we were eating Sally Babcock's scrumptious chicken gumbo. She makes it with okra and peppers, you know. But this year—" Agnes leaned forward, which sent the crystals dangling from her ear-lobes into lively motion "—she put shrimp in it."

She looked expectantly at Callie for a reaction.

Uncertain of the significance, Callie repeated, "Shrimp?"

"Yes, shrimp. I'm highly allergic to shrimp. So there I was, eating my gumbo, when my tongue and throat began to swell. I jumped up and hollered, 'Shrimp, shrimp!' but no one made a move to help me. Mr. Sullivan said I was turning purple. Ironic, since purple is my favorite color. Anyway, Jack Forrester showed up out of nowhere with his medical kit. He knows I'm allergic, you see. This happened before at his mother's house. She and I were good friends. Next-door neighbors, until Jack bought her house and she moved across the bay. Anyway, I yelled, 'shrimp!' and Jack gave me a shot."

"Antihistamine?"

Agnes nodded, but Grant muttered dryly, "I have my doubts."

Though she had already known of the allegation that Jack Forrester's injection had caused Agnes problems, the possibility that he'd administered the wrong medication filled Callie with inexplicable dread. Had he really made such a terrible mistake?

"What did he do then?" she asked. "Did he keep you under observation?"

"Oh, yes. He checked on me every few minutes for quite some time. The swelling in my throat and nose went away, and I could breathe again. I felt fine. *Very* fine, actually. Colors looked so bright and pretty, and every little noise sounded like music. It was lovely, just lovely. Mr. Sullivan and I took a stroll down the beach. How beautiful the sky and water looked!"

With a glance at the recorder, Grant interrupted her fond remembrance. "Get on with it, Mother."

"Oh…yes. Well, this part is hard to explain. I started seeing things. Fairies, dragons and big sunflowers with faces. Then my arms turned into butterfly wings. Yes, butterfly wings! Imagine my surprise. Of course I wanted to try them out, so I climbed up onto a sand dune. At the time, I thought it was a huge cocoon, you see. Then, I flew."

"You flew?"

"Yes, I flew. But not very far. The rest is all a jumble." She paused, looked down at her hand and continued in a subdued voice. "I woke up in the hospital with a sprained ankle, a concussion, and a—a—" a sheen welled up in her sky-blue eyes "—a shattered wrist."

Callie laid a gentle hand across hers. "That must have been terrible. It certainly sounds as if Dr. Forrester's injection had something to do with those hallucinations."

"Of course it did," Grant insisted. "Whatever he injected into Mother wasn't what it should have been."

"And yet, her allergic reaction subsided," Callie mused.

"No surprise there. Most of mother's 'allergic reactions' are entirely in her head. Psychosomatic. Forrester could have given her a sugar pill and alleviated her symptoms."

Agnes turned to him with a troubled look, as if she wanted to argue, but she held her tongue.

"Just to set the record straight, Ms. Marshall," he said, "there was no shrimp in Sally Babcock's gumbo."

Agnes sniffed and lifted her slightly jowled chin, her expression clearly indicating disagreement.

"I'll be sure to ask Sally about her gumbo," Callie said, conscious of a sudden tension between Agnes and Grant. "Did Dr. Forrester go with you to the hospital?" She couldn't imagine Jack not taking an active role in the crisis.

"No, he was out fishing, I believe," Grant answered. "He'd taken off on a boat shortly before Mother fell from the dune. He pays more attention to his fun and games than he does to the medication he injects into people."

Callie bit her lip. She could easily imagine Jack taking off in a boat. "Did the hospital offer an explanation for the hallucinations?"

"None. They did a whole battery of tests but came up with nothing. I have my doubts about their so-called tests, though. Jack Forrester works at that hospital. It only makes sense that they wouldn't want to incriminate one of their own."

"You think the hospital is withholding information?"

"I wouldn't doubt it."

Callie raised a brow and scribbled down a few notes. She would definitely check on those test results. Turning to Agnes, she asked, "Mrs. Tierney, forgive me, but…did you take any other medication that might have accounted for the hallucinations, or did you eat any strange foods that day, or…or smoke anything?"

"Absolutely not. I keep my body smoke-free and drug-free. I stick to a very rigid diet, too. I don't even eat red meat."

"Do you really think Mother would abuse any kind of substance?" Grant demanded with a quelling frown.

"No, of course not. But we do have to look for anything that could cause such a reaction. I'll have a doctor study your medical chart, Mrs. Tierney—with your permission, of course—along with the hospital tests."

"Any reasonable person can see that Jack Forrester's injection caused those hallucinations," Grant maintained. "My mother's injury has deprived her of her livelihood, as well as her lifelong passion—her art. I'd say it's only right that Jack Forrester pay."

"Does he have medical liability insurance?" Agnes asked, pressing a hand to her bosom. "I hope so. I'd hate to cause him *too* much trouble. He was always such a nice boy."

Callie was surprised by her concern.

Grant scowled. "Of course he has insurance, Mother, but that's beside the point. He caused you physical, emotional and financial distress, and if he ends up digging into his pockets, I'll be glad."

Agnes pursed her lips but offered no further comment. Callie resolved to speak to the woman alone, without her son's overbearing presence, as soon as possible. She obviously had reservations about pursuing this lawsuit—and, technically speaking, *she* was the plaintiff, not Grant. She would be the one testifying in court against Jack.

"Would you like tea, Miss Marshall?" she offered. "I have green, orange pekoe, Chinese, English and herbal from my very own garden."

"No, thank you, Mrs. Tierney. I really must be going, but I'd love to see you again sometime before I leave."

"You're coming to the picnic tomorrow, aren't you?"

"Picnic?"

"The Labor Day picnic. Everyone will be there. And I can introduce you to Mr. Sullivan. Bob Sullivan. We've become quite close, you know."

"Mother, I'm sure that Miss Marshall has more important things to do than hang around with the local yokels."

"Actually, the picnic might be a great place to talk to people," Callie reflected, somewhat offended by the expression "local yokels." She, after all, had grown up on the Point. Grant, on the other hand, had merely been a summer resident. "The crowd will basically be the same one that was at the July picnic, right?"

"Right!" Agnes exclaimed. "Exactly the same crowd."

"Maybe not exactly," countered Grant. "And it won't be easy to talk there, with all the hoopla going on. A waste of your time, I'd say."

"It'll be fun," Agnes pronounced. "And Grant needs a date. You'd be perfect for him."

"Mother!"

"He's single, you know," she confided to Callie. "Divorced. I barely had a chance to meet his ex-wife. The *third one*, that is. The other two I knew quite well. The first had been—"

"Mother, that's enough," Grant interjected. "Miss Marshall is too busy to chat." His face had turned a dull red. With a forced smile, he said to Callie, "Do you need a ride somewhere? I noticed that Dee from the bed-and-breakfast drove you here."

"My car is still stuck in the mud on Gulf Beach Road. The only tow truck on the Point wasn't available this morning, so Dee was kind enough to offer me a ride. But you don't have to drive me. Dee said I should just call her, and she'd come for me."

"Nonsense. I'd be delighted to drive you. Where to?"

"The inn, I suppose."

Before his mother could say more, Grant escorted Callie out to his plush luxury sedan. As they rode the short distance down the main highway to the Bayside Bed-'n-Breakfast, Callie thought about the possibility of Jack injecting Agnes with the wrong medication.

The very idea made her stomach hurt with apprehension. That reaction troubled her all the more. Why should she care if he'd grown so dangerously careless? He wasn't her concern.

Good Lord, was she hoping the plaintiff's allegations proved false? Of course not!

Grant turned his car between two palm trees and into the crushed-shell driveway of the cozy inn that overlooked the bay.

A glint of golden hair caught Callie's eye. A broad-shouldered figure stood in the driveway. His smile flashed brilliantly beside the savage scar on his sun-tanned face as he watched children skip through the sprinkler on the lawn.

Jack Forrester.

He was leaning against a tow truck.

"What the hell is *he* doing here?" Grant blurted angrily.

Callie couldn't have worded the question better herself. She also wondered how the tow truck had appeared at the inn. She'd tried to hire Bobby Ray Tucker's services this morning, but someone had borrowed his tow truck. Had that someone been Jack?

Before she'd unbuckled her seat belt, Grant had sprung from the car. She hurried to catch up to him as he stalked toward Jack, his footsteps crunching in the crushed-shell driveway.

With his dark, muscled forearms crossed over his powerful chest, Jack shifted his pleasant gaze away from the children playing in the yard to his approaching enemy. In patent unconcern, he looked past Grant to Callie. Looking utterly masculine in casual, tawny pants and a root-beer-brown shirt that perfectly matched his eyes, he directed the full power of his lazy smile at her. "Mornin', Ms. Marshall."

Their gazes connected, and an unexpected charge of attraction warmed her skin beneath her prim business clothes.

Before she could summon a suitably outraged voice, Grant demanded, "What are you doing here, Forrester?" He'd stopped a few prudent yards short of where Jack stood, but glared menacingly at him.

Jack's amiable expression didn't falter. "I'd say that's none of your business, Tierney."

"It is if you're here to harass Callie Marshall."

"I grew up harassing Callie Marshall. That's not about to change anytime soon."

Grant clenched his jaw and tightened his fists at his sides. In a navy-blue polo shirt, neat taupe trousers, an expensive gold watch and Italian loafers, he looked the epitome of moneyed elegance. Physically, he was almost as big as Jack, yet somehow seemed at a disadvantage against his muscular, nonchalant adversary.

"No amount of harassment will interfere with Callie's investigation," Grant informed him. Stopping just short of smugness, he added, "I assume you've heard that she and Meg are handling my case."

"I wasn't aware you *had* a case."

"You will be."

Callie stepped between the two men and glared at Jack. "Why are you here, Dr. Forrester?"

"Thought you might need a tow truck."

"You know damn well I do. Did you borrow it from Bobby Ray?"

"Yes, ma'am. Didn't want anyone else to get it before you did. Are you ready to go pull your car out of the mud?"

"She doesn't need your help to do that," Grant snapped.

"Are *you* going to do it for her?" A glint of amusement appeared in his brown eyes. "Sure you know how?"

A flush mottled Grant's aristocratic face. "Bobby Ray Tucker has more than enough experience with his tow truck to pull a car out of the mud. All it would take is a call to him."

"Yeah, but Bobby Ray doesn't have the truck at the moment. For the rest of the day—or however long I need it—it's mine."

"I'll find another one," Grant vowed, his lips stiff and white, "if I have to go all the way to town to get it."

"Better hurry." Jack glanced at the sky, which had darkened with clouds. "A storm's on the way. Once Gulf Beach Road gets saturated, there's no telling how long it might take before any kind of vehicle could get back there."

Callie heard Grant's teeth grinding...or maybe her own. "Are you offering to pull my car out of the mud, Dr. Forrester?"

"With pleasure, ma'am. All I ask is that you ride along with me. You know, to show me exactly where the car is. Wouldn't want to waste my valuable time looking for it."

"As if he couldn't find it," Grant scoffed. "Don't worry, Callie. I'll be following close behind in case you need me."

"Good luck." Again, amusement lit Jack's gaze. "If that pretty-boy car of yours gets mired down in muck, you might have quite a wait before you get it out. Personally, I wouldn't leave it in those woods for very long. You know how these local boys are. Might be stripped down to nothing overnight."

Worry zipped through Callie as she thought about her sister's Mercedes. An expensive car *would* be a temptation to the bored, rowdy teens around here, if her own childhood friends were anything to judge by. "Better not chance it, Grant."

"I'll borrow a four-wheel-drive from someone."

"You go do that," Jack urged.

"Come with me, Callie."

She cast a worried glance at the darkening sky. The heavy humidity of the sea air and the scent of impending rain warned her that time was short. "I really do need my car, Grant."

"You might also need the other few items I have for you, Ms. Marshall," Jack softly drawled.

Callie stiffened and shot him a quick glance.

Grant narrowed his eyes. "What other items?"

Jack lifted a brow, met Callie's gaze and remained pointedly silent. She knew which items he meant. She'd left her shoes, blouse and bra behind her when she'd stomped away from his boathouse yesterday. A sudden image of him dangling her bra in front of Grant Tierney brought a heated blush to her face. She hadn't told Grant that they'd been together, much less about the wound Jack had treated.

"Um, Grant…" Callie pulled him aside and whispered, "He's obviously trying to provoke you. Don't play his game. Whatever nonsense he has up his sleeve, I can handle it. Why don't you go home and—"

"Don't trust him, Callie. He's a cagey bastard, especially with women. He'll have you believing he's a persecuted saint and I'm the devil, if you give him half a chance."

She leveled him a forceful stare. "Mr. Tierney, do you trust me to handle this investigation properly, or not?"

"Well, yes, I do but—"

"If you have any reservations about my capability or my trustworthiness, let me know now and Meg will hire another investigator."

"It's not that I don't trust you. After all, you should know what a creep he is from the way he treated Meg."

Callie stared. "The way he treated Meg?" She hadn't known that anyone knew of her sister's past relationship with Jack, or his humiliating betrayal.

"Meg and I have been friends for years. I know how she feels about Jack. I assumed you felt the same way."

"My personal feelings about the defendant have nothing to do with the investigation." She didn't like the idea that he'd thought they would.

"Just don't let him talk you into forgetting how he—"

"Excuse me, Ms. Investigator," Jack called, "but we'd better hurry before the rain moves in."

With an anxious glance over her shoulder at Jack, she urged Grant, "Go. I need my car to finish the investigation, and he's my best chance of getting it."

Glaring at Jack one last time, Grant murmured to Callie, "Take everything he says with a grain of salt. And call me if there's a problem." He then strode stiffly down the driveway to his car.

She waited until he'd driven away before she turned

to Jack. They stared at each other, regrouping, in a silent assessment of what the other might be thinking.

They were, essentially, alone again.

Though the innkeeper's two young boys squealed as they ran through the sprinkler a short distance away and seagulls cried in forlorn notes from overhead, the silence between Jack and her took on a tense, intimate quality.

Jack was the first to move. Without a word or a smile, he opened the passenger door of the truck and gestured for her to get in.

She gripped the straps of her shoulder bag a little too tightly. "Why are you doing this?"

"I wanted the chance to apologize for last night." Gruffness had softened his voice, and a disturbing intensity filled his gaze. "And I want you to myself again."

Warmth invaded her. How could he affect her body temperature with only a few softly uttered words? The man was a danger. A true danger. "Why would you say something like that?" she admonished. "You know I can't go with you if you do."

"You wanted honesty."

"No." She shook her head, frightened by that honesty, and by how much she wanted to go with him anyway. "All I want is my car."

"I'll get it for you."

She twisted the straps of her shoulder bag nervously. It would be easy to slide into the truck beside him, to rationalize her need to do so. She *did* need her car, as well as the personal items she'd left at his boathouse.

Surely she could trust herself to handle any situation he might put her in. She might even turn the tables and learn more about him than he wanted her to know. She might actually further her investigation, get answers to some of the questions that had been bothering her since her conversation at the Tierneys.

Run away from him, Callie! an inner voice urged. *Run!* "Maybe I should wait for someone else's help."

"Maybe." The hint of a smile curved his mouth, though his golden-dark gaze had never looked more serious. "But don't," he whispered.

It lay there between them—the gauntlet he'd thrown down. *Dare you come with me? Can you spend any time at all in my company and still tell me I mean nothing to you?*

She understood the challenge better than he possibly could. He didn't know about the heat that coursed through her whenever he looked at her in that hot, possessive way—as he was looking now. He didn't know that she'd yearned for his kiss, once upon a time, back when they'd been only pals. He didn't know that she'd dreamed of him just last night, that she'd made slow, hard love to him and woken with his name on her lips.

She knew.

She had no business going with him. But she needed her car. She wanted her clothes back. She longed for answers to her questions. And she'd never walked away from a challenge thrown down by Jack Forrester.

Holding her chin at a haughty angle, she cut her gaze sharply away from his golden, scarred, beautiful face and climbed into the truck.

4

As a prim, silent Callie Marshall sat stiffly beside him in the tow truck, Jack forced his muscles to unclench and his hands to relax on the wheel.

He hadn't liked seeing her with Tierney.

He didn't like her taking Tierney's side against him.

He didn't like how much he disliked those things.

His reaction to Callie wasn't what it should be. Last night he'd lain awake analyzing that reaction—the blood-stirring desire that overcame him whenever she was near. Why did she affect him so strongly?

She'd grown into a beautiful woman, yes, but beautiful women weren't exactly a scarcity. They fluttered through his life like brightly colored butterflies. He'd never tried to hold on to one for too long. Never wanted to clip any wings.

He didn't have what it took to keep a woman happy beyond the bedroom. He needed his space, and time alone, and freedom to unwind whenever his work wrapped around his insides too tightly. Selfish though that might be, he had little left to give a woman, outside the bedroom.

He'd be crazy to go after Callie with sexual intent.

He wanted her as a friend. She'd shared the happiest part of his life. He'd known her better than he had his own sister, who was seven years younger than he. He'd spent more time with Callie than he had with his father, who'd been the local doctor, or his mother, a busy schoolteacher.

Until raging hormones had sent him in other directions, Callie had been there for him. She'd had a unique way of sharing. Other friends had shared the good times and the bad, adding their own brands of humor or pathos, but only Callie had tapped into his feelings, his reactions, his psyche. And he'd tapped into hers. Together they'd created an extra dimension to every situation. Extra laughs, challenges, discoveries, regrets.

Yesterday, for the first time in years, he'd felt that way again.

He wanted her back in his life. He wanted that extra spice in ordinary moments. He would do whatever it took to win her over. But he would not corrupt their friendship—or his chance to renew it, as slight as that chance seemed to be right now—by pursuing a sexual relationship.

He'd spent half the night reaching that decision.

He'd spent the other half imagining her hot and naked in his arms, in his bed. He'd imagined staring into her eyes while he made love to her.

Gripping the steering wheel harder, he blew out a long breath. He was doing it again. Wanting her. Wanting to stop the truck, pull her to him and kiss her into utter submission.

"Is this for me?"

The question drew his gaze to her. She held up the plastic bag he'd left on the seat, her dusky brows arched beneath dark, feathery bangs. She looked slim, neat and authoritative in her beige tailored suit. Unapproachable. Untouchable. All business. A challenge he'd have to ignore.

"Yeah," he replied. "It's for you."

She withdrew the contents from the bag. First came her leather pumps, rubbed free of mud but warped, with one heel missing. Next she retrieved her snagged silk blouse. "You've cleaned my shoes and blouse," she noted with surprise.

"The blouse came out okay."

"There's no stain." Surprise had replaced the wariness in her gray-green eyes.

"How's your injury this morning?"

"Fine. Much better."

"Think I should take another look at it?"

"No!" After gazing at him with something like alarm, she blushed then murmured, "But thank you for your concern. And for cleaning my blouse and shoes." She peered again into the empty bag, as if expecting another item to materialize. "What about... um—" she cleared her throat "—my bra?"

"That took extra soaking. It's still in my dryer."

Two little anxiety lines creased between her brows. "You didn't have to clean it. You could have stuck everything in a plastic bag and handed it over."

"You don't like the sight of blood, and I had laundry to do last night, anyway." He shrugged. "No big deal."

She caught her bottom lip between her teeth. A provocative thing for her to do—drawing his attention to her full, shapely mouth when he was trying not to think about kissing her.

He knew what she had on her mind, though. She didn't like the idea that he had her bra. She was probably envisioning ways he could embarrass her. "Want to stop by my house and get it?"

That, of course, wouldn't rate very high on her wish list. He could almost hear the debate raging inside her:

should she get the car before the rain began, or get her bra before he did something outrageous with it?

She crossed her arms and pursed her sulky, kissable mouth in a way that almost made him groan. "You're manipulative, Dr. Forrester."

"How so?"

"You know how. I shouldn't be with you, yet here I am, with you. And now I'm tempted to go to your house to get my bra back. I feel like a fly being lured into a spiderweb. *Step into my parlor,* said the big, old, scheming spider."

He couldn't help a slight smile at her dramatic interpretation. "And just what do you think I'd do to you once you were in my, uh, parlor?" His imagination supplied a wealth of stimulating possibilities.

"I don't know." She searched his face as if the answer lay encrypted there.

His desire for her stirred, along with hope. She had to feel something for him, or that hint of vulnerability wouldn't be glimmering in her eyes.

"Influence my investigation, maybe?" she guessed. *Not* one of the possibilities he'd been contemplating. "Discredit me? Compromise my sister's case?"

"I don't have to do any of those things, Callie. In fact, I intend to help you with this investigation. I didn't administer the wrong medication to Agnes, and I'd like to know why the hell she was hallucinating."

"Do you have any theories?"

"None worth mentioning."

"I'd like to ask you a few questions, but you might not want to answer without your attorney's approval."

"Are you warning me to be on my guard?" He threw her a pensive glance. "Why?"

"I'm only trying to be fair."

"The question is, has your definition of 'fair' changed?"

"What do you mean by that?"

"I have no doubt that you're a great investigator, Cal. Once you've latched onto a mystery, you dig until you have the answer. Like when someone kept robbing Bubba Scaggs's crab traps, or when a prankster put a snake in my mother's desk at school. You didn't rest until you came up with the truth." He tilted his head and gazed at her. "Do you still go after the truth, or do you just look for ways to build your case?"

The question hit Callie with uncanny force, and it took her a moment to respond. "I go for the truth." But she knew she wasn't being entirely honest. Though she looked for the truth as a matter of personal pride, she also gave the lawyers what they demanded: anything and everything they could possibly use against their target, whether it had a direct bearing on the case or not. She would cast a wide net, dragging for dirt. The lawyers would then cull through it to find their winning edge.

"If you look for the truth in this case, Callie, I have faith you'll find it."

She drew in a breath and glanced out her side window.

"Ask me," he urged. "Anything."

Although she wanted answers, she felt strangely hesitant. Slowly she took the cassette recorder from her purse. After recording his permission, she asked for his version of the incident. It matched Agnes's, although he'd described it with a good deal of medical jargon.

"Are you sure she was having an allergic reaction?"

"Of course."

"Because she said she was?"

"No, because I looked. Her mouth, tongue and throat were swelling. I've had to do tracheotomies on patients in similar situations, once their air passages were blocked. An injection usually relieves the symptoms, though. Which, in this case, it did. How could I have used the wrong medication when the symptoms subsided?"

Callie lapsed into reflective silence. The only way, of course, was if Grant was right and Agnes's "allergic reaction" had been imagined.

Jack narrowed his eyes on Callie's face. "Is there some question as to whether she was having an allergic reaction?"

"I'm simply playing the devil's advocate." She didn't intend to inform him of anything about Grant Tierney's stand. Meg would decide what Jack should know and when. "I want a clear understanding of the situation."

"Then clearly understand this. She could have suffocated without medical intervention."

"Were you her personal physician?"

"No. Tierney would never allow that."

"Does Agnes always follow Grant's wishes?"

"Always. She's afraid of his temper...with good cause."

Callie remembered the way Agnes had remained silent when Grant insisted her allergic reaction had been imagined. Had she been afraid to argue?

He'll have you believing he's a persecuted saint and I'm the devil himself, Grant had warned her. Was Jack trying to do precisely that—prejudice her against Grant?

For the sake of their recorded conversation, she changed the subject to pertinent facts. "Do you carry a variety of medications in your emergency kit, Dr. Forrester?"

"Some."

"Could any of them cause hallucinations?"

"Highly unlikely."

"I've learned that certain drugs for pain, sleep or seizures can cause hallucinations and come in injectible forms. Are you sure you don't carry those around with you?"

"I'm not a walking pharmacy, Cal."

"Doesn't it seem odd to you that the hospital didn't do a drug screen to find out why Agnes was hallucinating?"

"Because of her age, there are other factors that would be considered first. Like her head injury. They'd certainly run a brain scan and MRI. Then a blood chemistry to evaluate her hydration status and electrolytes. A blood count to check white blood cells. An X ray to rule out fluid on the lung. Too many natural causes are more likely to account for hallucinations in the elderly than substance abuse."

"But you'd given her an injection just before the hallucinations started. Wouldn't they logically connect that injection with the hallucinations?"

"The antihistamine I used would not cause hallucinations. Competent medical personnel know that."

Which brought them right back to where they'd started.

Callie looked away from him and realized that the rain had begun, and he'd turned on his wipers. Gulf Beach Road was only a short distance ahead, she knew. She turned off the recorder and tucked it into her purse.

"If you want to talk to the hospital staff, you're welcome to ride along with me," he offered. "I plan to be at the hospital for my afternoon rounds by one."

"Thank you, but I'd rather drive on my own, when I'm ready."

"Fine." He shrugged. "Just thought you'd get more cooperation from the staff if I introduced you." He allowed that truth to sink in. "If you'd like to talk to witnesses from the picnic, the Point is holding another one tomorrow. Everyone should be there."

"I know. I've been invited."

"Are you planning to go?"

"Maybe." She didn't intend to share her plans with him. Who knew what crazy plot he might hatch, given enough time?

"Most of our old gang will probably be there, too," he informed her. "Robbie, Jimbo, Francine."

"She goes by Francine now?"

"She tries. I still slip up and call her Frankie sometimes."

Nostalgia flashed through Callie. She hadn't seen or heard from her childhood friends in years. She'd tried keeping in touch, but after the first few letters and calls, life had become too hectic.

Jack slanted her a curious gaze. "Who invited you to the picnic?"

She smiled, remembering Agnes's enthusiastic invitation. Grant definitely hadn't seconded the idea that she come as his date, thank goodness. She wouldn't want him thinking she was romantically interested in him. "Agnes Tierney is trying her hand at matchmaking," she related with mild amusement. "She feels I'd be perfect for Grant, and asked if I'd like to—"

"What?" The word exploded from Jack's mouth more like a curse than a question, and the truck swerved slightly as he frowned at her. "You're going with Tierney?"

She blinked. "Well, I—"

"Damn it, Callie, you'd better not be. You'd better not even be considering it."

She stared at him, stunned by his reaction. "Pardon me?"

"Tierney is bad news. Finish whatever business you have, then stay the hell away from him."

Her bafflement grew, along with her ire. She hadn't tolerated commands like that from the Colonel; she certainly wouldn't from Jack. "Are you trying to tell me with whom I may or may not socialize?"

"It's for your own good. I've seen what he can do to a woman, and I—"

"Don't patronize me, Dr. Forrester. I can take care of myself, and I'm not your concern. And stop trying to paint Grant Tierney as a villain. He warned me that you'd try."

Jack's mouth compressed into a thin white line of fury. "If you go with him, Callie, I swear, I'll take you away from him. I'll physically pick you up and carry you off."

Her jaw dropped. "You can't threaten me with force! I'd have you arrested so quickly it would make your head spin."

He cursed beneath his breath, bore down on the brake and swung the truck around on the shoulder of the road and into a sharp U-turn, throwing her against the door.

"What are you doing?" She clung to a side handgrip as he accelerated.

He didn't answer, his gaze trained on the road, his

jaw tightly clenched and a vein throbbing at his temple.

"Jack, the rain is getting worse. If you've changed your mind about helping me get my car, then at least—"

"Don't worry about the rain. It would have to pour for a week to stop a tow truck from getting to your car." He didn't look the least repentant for having led her to believe otherwise. "For now, there's something you're going to see, damn it."

The force of his fury shocked her. She'd never seen him this angry. He steered the truck off the main road and down a graveled pathway through the woods. The greenery soon opened up and she recognized the landscaped yard and the wood-sided ranch house built high on sturdy pilings.

His house. The one he'd grown up in.

An exuberant black-and-tan German shepherd bounded up to the truck with a welcoming canine smile, tail wagging and tongue lolling. He reminded Callie of Thor, the dog Jack had raised from a puppy when they'd been kids.

This couldn't be Thor, though. He'd be too old by now. Something like homesickness assailed Callie. Thor had been the pet she'd never owned. She'd missed him without realizing it.

Jack pulled the truck into the garage beneath the house, out of the rain that beat down in torrents. With a brief tousle of the dog's head and a curt command to "Stay, Zeus," Jack strode around to Callie's door and yanked it open. "Come with me."

She knew better than to argue. At the very least, it would delay them from retrieving her car. And she was undeniably curious about the cause of his anger and what he had to show her. Ignoring vague qualms about spending too much time alone with him, she followed Jack up the covered stairway, through the front entrance and into the spacious great room.

She paused inside, struck by the sudden warmth of familiarity. Very little seemed to have changed. A massive stone fireplace dominated the front wall, surrounded by the same cozy armchairs and sofas. A low, wide counter separated the back corner into a sleek kitchen that still contained two oversize refrigerators. One had always been stocked with food, the other with beverages. Across from the kitchen, a wooden table with six immense captain chairs sat beside an old-fashioned jukebox.

They'd played a lot of card games at that table. Listened to a lot of music. Drunk a lot of sodas.

Behind the table, a floor-to-ceiling window overlooked the beach and the silvery green waters of the Gulf of Mexico. This particular view seemed more familiar to her than the city park below her Tallahassee apartment.

She half expected Jack's mother, father, sister or cousins to round the corner from the bedrooms or the back porch with a friendly hello. No one did. They were alone.

Jack swept her forward with a firm hand at the small of her back, ushering her to the right of the main living area and into the master bedroom suite.

Even this room generated a nostalgic warmth. When the big television in the great room had been otherwise engaged, she and Jack and other friends had sprawled out on the king-size bed, the cushiony chairs and the carpeted floor to watch the television built high into the bedroom wall at just the right angle for mass viewing. Side tables had always borne trays of snacks or bowls of popcorn and drinks.

Callie's chest grew tight at the memories. Nowhere had she felt more at home. Not even at her father's house. *Especially* not at her father's house.

"Sit," Jack told her, pointing at the bed. He softened the curt command with, "Please."

She considered objecting, decided against it and sat on the very edge of the bed. "Do your parents still live here?"

"No." Though his handsome, scarred face still looked taut with angry determination, he added, "I bought the house from them. They wanted something smaller." He opened a closet, pulled out a crate and set it on a nearby armchair.

Highly curious, Callie watched him rifle through papers and envelopes. What could he possibly want to show her? Something to do with Grant Tierney, obviously. She couldn't even hazard a guess as to what it might be.

He drew out envelopes of loose photographs, strode to the bed and sat down beside her. Briskly he flipped through the photos and tossed a few onto her lap.

"You and Grant," she noted in surprise, lifting each photo to examine it. She saw two young friends grinning and clowning for the camera. Pals.

"We went to the same college. I got to know him pretty well. Or so I thought." He handed her another photo.

A wedding picture.

"Becky." She peered in admiration at the lovely, glowing young bride in the photo. She was blond like Jack, but with wide-set blue eyes. His younger sister. Callie's gaze then shifted to the groom. "And Grant!"

"She married him the day she turned eighteen. He was twenty-seven. It didn't take long for things to turn bad."

"If his marriage with your sister didn't work out, I can understand why you might hold a grudge against him, but I'd rather not discuss it. Frankly, it's none of my business."

"Look at this, Callie," Jack ordered fiercely, pushing a photo into her hands.

At first, she didn't recognize the haggard, rail-thin woman in the photo. After a moment, though, she realized it was Becky, her face pale and drawn with dark circles under her eyes and a haunting bleakness in her expression.

"What happened to her?" Callie whispered, horrified.

"Tierney happened to her, that's what. After the wedding, he became pathologically possessive. He forbade her to have any contact whatsoever with family or friends. Kept her a virtual prisoner. She was afraid to tell anyone how bad it was—even me. After two hellish years of marriage, she needed four years of therapy to bring her back to life."

Callie closed her eyes in sympathy for the girl she'd once loved as a little sister. Glumly she handed the photo back to Jack. She didn't know what to say, what to think. Could he possibly be lying about this to portray Grant in a bad light, as Grant had predicted he would? The photo itself proved nothing. Any number of things could have caused the change in Becky.

Yet, Callie believed Jack. He wouldn't lie about something like this. She would never look favorably on Grant Tierney again.

Her disapproval of him, however, would make no

difference to her investigation of the malpractice suit. She worked for Meg and would do her best to help her prepare the case. Grant's personal life didn't enter into it at all. "Where's Becky now?"

"Living halfway across the continent. She doesn't want anyone from the Point to know her location. She's afraid Tierney might wheedle it out of someone and come after her."

"Do you think he would?"

"He stalked her after the divorce, if that's what you mean. Threatened her. Said he'd never let her go."

"How frightening for her." Struck with a sudden thought, Callie searched Jack's face. "Did you...do anything?" she asked, almost afraid to hear. "To stop him, I mean, or to retaliate?"

"He didn't listen to warnings." He lifted his wide shoulders in a casual shrug. "So I beat the hell out of him." A muscle moved in his jaw. "He gave up stalking for a while, but he also had the sheriff pick me up for assault. The charge didn't stick, though. No witnesses. He had no proof."

She wished he hadn't told her. An assault charge, even if it hadn't "stuck," was just the kind of dirt she was being paid to gather about him. Anything to make a jury dislike him. Anything that might tarnish his name and force him to settle.

"After Becky left Tierney, he married another woman," Jack said. "She divorced him, too. I know from mutual friends that he treated her the same way. The third time he went to marry, I warned the bride."

"The *bride?*" Callie repeated. "You can't mean...at the wedding itself!"

"There wasn't any way around it. I didn't know her, or how to get in touch with her before the wedding, but

I couldn't let another woman blindly throw herself into that hell. It turned out that she hadn't known about his first two wives at all, before I'd mentioned it. She called off the wedding and asked me to drive her home from the chapel."

"Grant must have been furious."

A sardonic twist of his mouth sent a chill down her back. "You could say that."

His gaze held hers, and a suspicion gripped her. "The scar." Her hand involuntarily rose, her fingers feathering over the jagged white line on his cheek, as if the puckered texture within his smooth-shaven face could possibly tell the story. "And there's one on your shoulder, too," she recalled. "I saw it yesterday, when you took off your shirt."

Darkness flickered through his gaze, and his jaw squared.

"What happened?" she demanded, suddenly feeling sick, shaken and inexplicably angry—at him, at Tierney, at everyone.

"The scars are nobody's business."

She angrily rose from the bed. "I figured they were from something stupid you'd done," she lashed out. "And I was right. For God's sake, Jack...stopping the man's wedding! Leaving with his bride! You're lucky he didn't shoot you."

Jack's expression didn't change.

That very fact alerted her. She felt her own eyes widen and her face drain of warmth. "Did he? Did he shoot you?"

He frowned in annoyance and stood up with a cool, dismissive air. "As far as I'm concerned, these scars don't exist. We won't talk about them again."

His sudden refusal to answer her questions distracted her from her anger. She'd obviously hit a nerve. "You're well aware they exist, or you wouldn't mind talking about them." Her prodding only succeeded in tightening his jaw to granite hardness. "If the scars bother you that much, why don't you have them surgically removed?"

"Damn it, Callie, they don't bother me. But since you've asked, my surgeon pals did all they could. And they did a damn fine job. But I guess their magic wands didn't work as well as you feel they should have."

She stared at him in stark dismay. She hadn't meant to imply that the scars bothered her. They did, but only because of the pain, the danger, the life-threatening conflict they represented. If the surgeons had done all they could and the scars were still visible, he must have been grievously injured. She couldn't bear to think about what he'd gone through, and yet she couldn't stand not knowing. "Please tell me what happened."

"The subject is closed."

She'd never known him to clam up like this. She sensed deep, dark emotion swirling just beneath his surface. Ignoring his cold, forceful words, she peered past his anger, trying to divine the feelings he hadn't expressed. "You won't acknowledge those scars or tell anyone how you got them," she guessed, "because you don't want to admit he permanently marked you."

Surprise flashed through his gaze, and she knew she'd read him correctly.

"The scars haven't hurt you, Jack," she pressed on, sensing a crack in his armor. "I'm sure the women still go crazy over you, like they always have. Probably more so."

"Drop it, Cal," he warned. "I don't need your pep talk."

"Jack!" She caught his rugged face between her palms and held him tightly. "Your anger at Tierney must be horrendous. Don't bottle it up and refuse to talk about it, or it'll scar you in the worst way—on the inside." She stared at him with earnest concern flowing straight from her heart.

He absorbed the message, it seemed, but somehow delved deeper than she'd expected, beyond her words, to the chaotic, vulnerable place where they'd originated.

The moment grew too poignant. She slowly lowered her hands from his face, feeling shaken.

He let out a short, rough breath. Closed his eyes, opened them. "As pesky as you are," he whispered, "I can't believe how damn much I've missed you."

Warm emotion crowded her chest and blurred her vision. She wanted to say she hadn't missed him, but he would know she lied. She wanted to turn away and dodge the issue. She wanted, more than anything, to kiss him. "We can't be friends," she said, her whisper heavy with regret.

He swept his hand up the curve of her face in a lingering caress. His voice grew thick and soft. "Then what *can* we be?"

She didn't have an answer.

In a gruff whisper, he swore, "I'll take anything I can have of you."

Their gazes intensified. His strong, hard fingers slipped into her hair. He leaned in and touched his mouth to hers. A light, tentative touch. Barely a kiss. But he stayed there, sustaining that feather-light con-

tact, his eyes closed, his warm, heart-pounding stillness a silent plea for more.

Sensuality radiated from their lightly joined lips to
the most intimate hollows of her body. She inhaled
slowly, deeply, savoring his heat, his scent, his nearness, until the urge for more overpowered her.

She wasn't sure who moved first, who began the seductive brush of mouth against mouth, the slow, gliding tastes, the nibbles and tugs, the thrust of tongues.

A strange, hot magic possessed her.

She pressed closer, needing to satisfy a sudden craving. Her arms slid around his muscled shoulders. Her
fingers dug into the thick, silky hair at his nape, and
she plunged into the keen pleasure of his kiss.

The kiss grew hotter, deeper, rougher.

A groan tore from Jack's throat as a powerful need
burgeoned within him. He'd fantasized about this for
so long. Kissing, tasting, savoring these very lips.
Holding this very woman. Making love to her.

Good Lord, he wanted to. Needed to.

He ran his hands beneath her suit jacket, up and
down her slender back and curvaceous sides, hungry
for her softness. Her low moan vibrated through their
kiss, and she rocked her hips in sensual response to his
caresses.

His blood heated. His hands coursed down to her
backside and cupped her against him, lifting her for a
closer fit.

"Jack," she whispered against his mouth, sounding
worried, "I'm not being fair to you. I should stop now
instead of leading you on, making you think there's
any chance that I might—"

"Let me worry about what's fair." He kissed her
again, angling for deeper access. She welcomed him

with silken heat and a sinuous movement of her body that made him groan.

"I'll be stopping soon," she warned in a throaty murmur.

He gazed into her slightly dazed green eyes and nipped at her voluptuous bottom lip. "Okay."

They came together in another deep, moving kiss. He pressed her against him in every way he could, craving the feel of her. A low, pleasured sound rolled from her throat, and his need intensified into an ache.

He pulled her down onto the bed, kissing her face, her jaw, her neck.

"Jack," she said in a shaky whisper, lying now beneath him, "you understand I'm going to stop, don't you?"

"No," he breathed. He drew his tongue along her jaw, and when he reached her ear, whispered, "I don't understand it."

She closed her eyes with a sexy groan and arched her long, slender throat, enticing him into a downward path. "There's no way I can get involved with you."

Losing himself in the subtle wildflower fragrance of her hair and the alluring feminine scent that was only Callie's, he took his time sampling the taste and texture of her skin.

She skimmed her hands along his back and made small, writhing movements of her body, inflaming him.

He pushed her suit jacket off her shoulders and searched for buttons on her blouse. Frustration rose within him. The damn thing buttoned in the back. He took the edge off of his urgency by returning to her mouth. She met him in a hot, passionate kiss.

He ran his hands over her breasts, cupping and

kneading through the interfering silk and lace, rousing her nipples to hardness. He'd seen her breasts yesterday. He'd spent half the night remembering. He wanted to take each dark, flowery crest into his mouth and make her burn for him—

"Jack!" She stopped him with a breathy gasp as he reached behind her to unbutton her blouse. Her eyes shone with sensuality and her face blazed with color. "I'm going to leave here and conduct an investigation against you. Nothing we've said or done will change that. I'm going to gather every miserable piece of dirt I can find to blacken your name—"

He stopped her with another kiss.

She punished him in a skirmish of tongues, of bodies, shoving him away while drawing him in deeper, arching against him but deflecting his hands in a sensuous wrestling match that soon gave way to mutual passion.

His hand traversed the length of her—breast, waist, hip, thigh. She writhed beneath his touch like a cat being petted. He pushed her skirt up to savor the hot satin smoothness of her thigh.

"No, wait," she panted, trapping his hand. "You have to listen. I misled you before, Jack. I'm not only going after the truth about this case. I'm going after dirt. *Dirt.*"

She nudged his hand off her thigh and tugged her skirt back into place.

With her silky dark hair tousled from his fingers plowing through it, her mouth puffy and glistening from his roughhouse kisses and her green eyes stormy with emotion, she was so beautiful it hurt to look at her.

It would hurt more to let her go and know he

couldn't kiss her again. It would probably kill him to watch her work to destroy his name.

But he'd learned over the course of his career how to deflect all manner of pain, in himself and others. How to treat the worst of cases and turn off his caring, his hope, his frustration, his grief, whenever the job was done. He'd taken that hard-earned skill with him into his personal life, and he put it to good use now.

"Dirt, did you say?" He lifted a brow. "I love it when you talk dirty." He dropped a kiss alongside her jaw.

She groaned and shoved against his chest. "You're not taking me seriously."

He propped up on his elbow and stared down at her. She had no idea how wrong she was. He'd never taken a woman *more* seriously. She intended to remain aloof despite the deep, hot kisses that had set him on fire like none ever had. He took that very seriously, indeed.

He intended to make love to her.

"You think you're so tough, don't you?" he scoffed lightly, tugging at a wavy tendril of her hair.

She rose up on one elbow to confront him eye-to-eye. "As a matter of fact, I do."

"If you're so tough, then what we do here shouldn't matter, since it has nothing to do with the case."

Her dark brows drew together. "You would make love to me knowing that I'm going to try to destroy your reputation?"

His pulse sped up at the very mention of making love to her. "Yes."

"Which means—" her gaze skittered away from his "—it wouldn't mean anything to you, either."

He frowned. He hadn't said that. How the hell did she put words in his mouth? He hooked a finger beneath her chin and turned her face toward his. "I told you before, Callie. I'll take anything I can have of you."

Their gazes clashed. The silence grew taut.

"Why?"

She couldn't have posed a harder question. He didn't know the answer. He'd convinced himself earlier that he wanted her friendship, and that sexual involvement would destroy his chance of renewing it. But that had been before he'd kissed her. Before he'd known about the sweet, hot passion that burned away every doubt, leaving only a gut-wrenching need for her.

He ran his thumb slowly across her voluptuous mouth. Her breath caught. Her eyelids fluttered. A pulse began to beat in her throat. He knew she would let him kiss her again, and his voice went hoarse with desire. "A better question is, *why not?*"

His logic, it seemed, won her over. She met him halfway. No sooner had his lips grazed hers than the telephone rang. The pattern of the rings alerted him to a call forwarded from his answering service.

An emergency.

He shut his eyes, wanting to curse. Why now? Why, when his gut was telling him the time was right to make her forget every scruple?

He pulled away from her, muttered a curse and answered his bedside phone.

Callie let out a shaky breath and collapsed on his bed. She'd literally been saved by the bell. What had she been thinking? She *hadn't* been thinking. She'd been responding mindlessly to his potent allure and her own wicked desire.

She had to get the hell away from him.

She scrambled from the bed and searched for her purse and shoes, unsure of what she'd done with them.

"Calm down. Take a deep breath," Jack ordered. It took her a moment to realize he was speaking into the phone. "Is she breathing? Good. Conscious? Good." He held the receiver in the crook of his neck while he buttoned his shirt and tucked its tails into the waistband of his tan trousers. "Don't move her. I'll call an ambulance. Yes, I'll be there, too."

He hung up the phone, then placed a call to the paramedics, rattling off medical information about the patient as he snatched his key ring from the dresser.

Callie slipped into her shoes, adjusted her clothing and peered into his dresser mirror. Quickly she freshened the lipstick that had been kissed away and combed the tangles from her hair. Her linen suit was sadly wrinkled, as if she'd been sleeping in it. Or making love in it. Her heart turned over at the thought. She'd almost made love to Jack Forrester!

Shaking herself to dispel maverick emotions that only confused her more, she tried to smooth the wrinkles out of her suit. She'd wanted to present a competent, businesslike image to the community. Perhaps she should return to the inn and change before continuing with her investigation.

The realization then hit her that she didn't have a car. Her sister's Mercedes was still stuck in the mud. She glanced at her watch, hoping that Dee from the inn might drop by and pick her up. But Dee had mentioned she wouldn't be available after noon, and it was now twelve-fifteen.

"Mrs. Sanchez fell on the stairs," Jack told her, setting down the phone. "Sounds like she might have broken her hip."

Callie turned to him in concern. "Mrs. Sanchez? Gloria's mother?"

"The one and only. Best guacamole and tortilla chips on the Point. I doubt if she'll be making them anytime soon, though." He ushered Callie out of the bedroom with a hand at her waist. Even that casual touch sent warmth spiraling through her. "I won't have time to pull your car from the mud right now."

"Of course not."

"I'd let you have the tow truck, but Bobby Ray wouldn't want anyone else driving it." He paused in the great room, near the front door, and eyed her uneasily. "I'd offer you my car, but my medical supplies and equipment are in the trunk. I'm not sure what I'll need of it."

"No, no, I wouldn't take your car." She didn't want to risk interfering with his treatment of Mrs. Sanchez in any way. Besides, how could she explain to the community why she was driving Jack Forrester's car?

"You're welcome to stay here," he offered. "Freddie and the Flounders should be dropping by soon to rehearse for tomorrow's picnic. Their wives won't let them practice at their houses, so they use mine. A little music might liven up your afternoon."

"My afternoon's been livened up quite enough already, thank you." She didn't want to be caught at Jack's house by anyone, or rumors would surely fly. "No offense to Freddie or his Flounders, but I'd rather not stay."

"That leaves you with one option. My Harley."

"Your Harley!"

"I wouldn't particularly recommend it. It's pretty big. Might be hard for you to handle, especially in the rain." He paused and gave the matter another thought.

"Then again, you *would* make for an interesting sight."
His gaze meandered down to the slim skirt he'd
pushed up her thighs only moments ago.

Her pulse quickened. "Of course I can't take your
Harley."

He shrugged, reached into the closet and drew out
an umbrella. Only the slightest of smiles lit his golden-
brown eyes. "Then it looks like you're coming with
me."

5

IF SHE HAD KNOWN where Mrs. Sanchez now lived, Callie would have walked the four or five miles to the inn through the rain in her high heels rather than accompany Jack on his emergency call.

Too late, she realized the call would take them to the neighborhood where she'd grown up. He turned his sports car down the narrow, asphalt road where a tidy row of homes edged the bayside canal. The yellow cinder-block house in the middle of the row had been the Colonel's house.

When her mother had been alive, she'd thought of it as home, although the Colonel's strict rules and critical eye had always prevented her from feeling truly at ease there.

She stiffened in the luxurious leather seat of Jack's expensive car as they slowly drove through her old neighborhood. She hadn't ventured anywhere near the place in twelve years. Not that she hadn't been tempted, so many times, to choke down her pride and pay her stern, autocratic father a visit.

It was too late now, of course. The Colonel had passed away last year.

"I'd forgotten we'd be in your old neighborhood," Jack remarked. "Mrs. Sanchez lives about four doors down from the Colonel's old place."

Callie didn't reply as they drove by her childhood home.

"A couple with three kids live there now."

She found that somewhat comforting. At least the place had life now. The presence of a trampoline, a tricycle and a football in the front yard testified to the change. The Colonel had never allowed any playthings to clutter his neat front lawn.

Jack sent her a searching glance. "Did you ever mend your rift with him?"

Unexpected tightness swelled around her vocal chords, making it difficult to answer. "A few months after I left, I called him. He accepted my apology for, uh, insubordination."

Jack smiled a little at that. "Then why didn't you visit?"

"I wasn't invited." She tried to keep her tone light but didn't quite succeed. "He dropped by to see Meg and me a couple of times in Tallahassee. Or rather, to inspect our quarters." She forced a rueful smile. "But whenever we mentioned visiting him, he discouraged it. He always had other plans."

She looked away to hide the pain sifting through her. He really hadn't wanted her in his life. "Oh, don't think he neglected us. He offered to pay our bills and give us cash. But I, uh…" She didn't finish. No one needed to know that she'd refused his financial help. She'd wanted to force him into a choice, as he'd forced her: Give me a place in your heart, in your life, or cut the ties. He'd cut ties.

She felt Jack's gaze on her. "You heard about the fishing boat he bought, didn't you?" he asked. She shook her head, too unsure of her voice to speak. "A nice one," he recalled. "He had it for years, but when he moved overseas, he had to sell it."

Callie frowned, unsure of his point.

"He named it *The Colonel's Callie*."

She stared at him, incredulous. He'd named his boat after *her*? The idea shook her. Stunned her.

"He had a smaller bass boat that he'd named *The Lady Meg*." Jack pulled the car over to the side of the road and parked it. With a gruff, earnest softness, he said, "Some people are just afraid to love, Cal, or else they don't know how. It doesn't mean they don't feel it."

She looked sharply away from him. She couldn't think about the Colonel now—or the incredible news that he'd acknowledged her, in some small way, as a part of him. "It's history," she whispered. "Doesn't matter anymore."

"I believe it does."

"I don't want to talk about this, Jack, just like you don't want to talk about those scars on your face."

"I'd say that's an excellent comparison." His tone drew her gaze back to his. "Tierney pulled a gun on me while he was in a rage. I tried to take it away from him, and it went off." After a pause, he added, "Whenever you're ready to tell me about *your* scars, I'll be ready to listen."

Her scars. She supposed she did have a few. But now was not the time or place to discuss them.

Needing to change the subject, she gestured toward the A-frame home where they'd stopped. "Is this Mrs. Sanchez's?"

"Yeah."

"The ambulance hasn't arrived yet."

"We had a shorter distance to drive. It'll take the ambulance another thirty minutes, coming from the hospital."

She understood then why folks on Moccasin Point would call Jack instead of the paramedics in an emergency. In certain situations, the ambulance would arrive too late.

"Should I wait in the car?" she asked.

"You can, but I wish you'd come in." He reached behind the seat and brought out a black leather doctor's bag. "Never know where you might be needed."

An odd little pang of gratification warmed her at the thought that she might be needed. Bemused by her unusually sensitive emotional state, Callie followed Jack across the yard. In Tallahassee, she'd acquired a reputation for cool reserve. Her associates and employees often kidded her about it. She'd been feeling anything but "cool" or "reserved" lately.

A petite brunette in her late thirties rushed out of the house to meet Jack. Gloria. As a vivacious teenager, she'd been Callie and Meg's favorite baby-sitter. Though a little rounder and considerably older, she looked basically the same.

"Oh, Doc, I'm so glad you're here." Her dark eyes were red-rimmed, her face splotchy. "I didn't know Mama was on the stairs. I heard this terrible *thump-thump*, and she called out for me." Her face crumpled. "She's l-lying there in so much p-pain." She covered her eyes with her hand and wept.

Two little girls hovering in the doorway chimed in with noisy sobs. From somewhere inside, a baby wailed.

Jack's arm went around Gloria as he escorted her into the house, his golden head tipping close to hers.

"Calm yourself, Glo. You're scaring the kids, and probably your mother, too."

With a dismayed exclamation, she halted her crying, glanced at her teary-faced toddlers and veered toward them. Jack strode through the small living room to the foot of the stairs. Callie stopped a discreet distance behind him, feeling awkward and intrusive, although no one had given her so much as a glance.

Jack knelt beside the thin woman in a faded housedress who lay at an awkward angle on her side. Though valiantly silent, she breathed in shallow gasps, her forehead beaded with sweat. Her dark, pain-glazed eyes locked with his.

"Rosa, Rosa, didn't I tell you not to cha-cha down those stairs?" His tone, his smile, conveyed a calm friendliness that somehow eased Callie's tension and won a weak, pained smile from his patient. His hands, meanwhile, moved over her frail-looking body in a steady, methodical manner. "Where does it hurt?"

She murmured a reply. He asked more questions, held her hand and bent closer to examine her more thoroughly.

A telephone rang. The baby cried from a back room. Gloria herded the girls and an older boy into the kitchen.

Callie ventured into a bedroom, toward the sound of the baby's crying. She found a burly little boy standing in forlorn solitude, his dimpled fists gripping the rail of the crib, his chubby cheeks slick with tears. She smiled and murmured a friendly greeting. He reached for her. Absurdly pleased, she swung him into her arms, and his sobs subsided.

He cuddled against her with sweet, trusting innocence. She thought of Meg's two children at his age, which had been eight and nine years ago. She'd been too immersed in building her business to spend much time with them.

She couldn't afford to regret that. Her business generated enough income to build a solid future for herself, to insure her independence. Nothing could be as important. But as she held the soft, powder-scented baby and pressed her cheek against his head, she wished she'd spent more time with her niece and nephew.

An ambulance siren grew steadily louder until it screamed to a halt outside. Callie stepped into the hallway and peered into the living room, which now teamed with uniformed men. Jack remained at Rosa's side and spoke with the emergency team.

Gloria skirted around the hubbub of activity and bustled toward Callie. "Callie? Callie Marshall? Is that you?"

She'd wondered if Gloria would recognize her.

They barely had time to exchange more than a few pleasant exclamations before Gloria's grandson tugged at her denim skirt and threatened to throw up. She hurried him into the bathroom and the other toddler ran along to watch.

Stimulated by the activity, the baby in Callie's arms squirmed, arched and squealed to be let down. She struggled to maintain a firm hold. She soon realized with dismay that he needed a dry diaper. It wasn't easy, carrying the zestful one-year-old to his nursery, finding a fresh diaper and wrestling him down onto the changing table to do the deed. With a cloth diaper, no less.

As she fought to keep a grip on the playful baby, fold the diaper and pin it on him properly, a pair of large, sun-bronzed hands reached around her, held the baby's hips neatly down and slid the pin into perfect position.

Hedged in by masculine arms and a muscular chest, Callie craned her neck to look up into Jack's smiling brown eyes. "I could have done it myself, you know," she said.

"Sure you could have." He placed a bright yellow teething ring into the baby's chubby hands, which drew a squeal of delight and thoroughly distracted him from his escape attempts.

Callie lifted the contented baby into her arms and sidestepped Jack to cut him a wry glance. "You can wipe that smirk off your face now."

"What smirk?"

"The one that says—"

"He's drooling on your shoulder."

"That's not what I was going to—oh!" She drew back and examined a wet stain that had spread across her beige suit. She laughed and hugged the baby closer. "I've already given up on this suit for today, anyway."

Jack studied her with something like surprise, then pivoted to gaze at the baby's face. "I've been trying to get this woman to laugh for two days now, Bud. You've done it in less than an hour. I'll have to remember the drooling trick."

Callie laughed again, feeling somewhat protected from Jack's winsome charm. He couldn't possibly entice her into an unwise kiss or embrace while she clung to the baby. "I'm not sure if you could pull it off with the same effect."

"Uh-oh, bud." Jack continued to eye the baby. "Now you're biting her shoulder. Moving in on *my* territory."

A ridiculous warmth flooded her, and before she could rebuke him for saying nonsensical things that could give others a wrong impression, Jack had shifted to meet her gaze with a smile so warm she couldn't speak. She realized then that *nothing* could protect her from his devastating charm.

"Will she be okay, Doc?" Gloria's anxious voice from the bedroom doorway startled Callie. "Is Mama's hip broken?"

"Looks more like she's dislocated it. But I want to run tests at the hospital to be sure. They're putting her in the ambulance now. I'm going to ride along with her."

Callie glanced at him in surprise. She hadn't expected that. She was glad, though. Mrs. Sanchez had seemed comforted by his presence.

"I'm glad you'll be there, Doc," Gloria said. "I can't go to the hospital with Mama until my husband gets home from work."

Callie followed Jack with the baby in her arms as he walked with Gloria, answering her questions and uttering reassurances. When they reached the front yard, Gloria took the baby from Callie and profusely thanked her and Jack.

"I hope I didn't ruin any plans you had for today." Her earnest gaze shifted from Jack to Callie.

"Oh, we didn't have plans," Callie hurriedly assured her. "I mean, *I* didn't. Except business. Just business. That's the only reason I'm here. With Jack, I mean. We're not…he's not—"

Jack smoothly interrupted, "I'm glad you called me, Gloria. I have to be at the hospital this afternoon, anyway. I'll be admitting your mother for at least a couple days."

Gloria thanked him again and headed for the ambulance, where the paramedics were lifting her mother on a stretcher.

"Take my car, Callie," Jack said. "I won't need it. I have a knee replacement at two o'clock, ankle surgery at five, a cast to remove and rounds to make. I'll catch a ride home from the hospital and pull your car out of the mud when I get off work this evening."

"You don't have to do that." For some odd reason, the seriousness of his work had only recently hit her—seeing him tending to Mrs. Sanchez, hearing the surgeries he'd be performing. He'd somehow transformed from the infuriating tease she'd always known into a bonafide doctor. She suddenly felt awkward, expecting him to tow her car from the mud after a day of saving lives and limbs. "I'll find someone else," she insisted.

"I'll do it. Tonight." He turned her toward his car and urged her forward. "I'm not sure what time, but I'll bring your car to the inn, and we'll switch vehicles."

"No, I'll call Bobby Ray Tucker. Maybe he can drop by your house, get the tow truck and pull my car out of the mud."

"He and his family are leaving town today for the long weekend. That's why he let me have the tow truck." They'd reached his car. He opened the driver's door for her and handed her his key. "Give me your key. I'll haul your car out of the mud, tow it to my house, leave the truck there and drive your car to the inn."

Despite her misgivings, she really had no choice but to take him up on his offer. Hesitantly she gave him her key, then slid behind the wheel of his car. "I hate for you to go through all this trouble. I mean, I know you

brought it on yourself by borrowing the tow truck before I had the chance to call Bobby Ray—'' she shot him
an admonishing glance ''—but you'd planned to use it
this morning, and now you'll have to wait until after a
shift at the hospital. You'll be tired, and maybe it'll be
dark by then.''

''I'll charge you for my trouble.'' Instead of shutting
the car door, he rested his arm on the roof and smiled
down at her.

''Charge me what?''

''A modest fee.''

''Hey, Doc,'' yelled a paramedic from the ambulance. ''We'll be ready to go in a few minutes.''

''Thanks. I'll be right there.'' He glanced at Callie
with an unsettling warmth in his gaze. ''I'll charge you
two kisses.''

''What?''

He leaned in and lightly kissed her mouth. ''See you
tonight,'' he whispered.

Before she could shake off the surprised daze
enough to protest, he shut the door and strode toward
the ambulance. Halfway up the driveway, he looked
back at her. ''That leaves an unpaid balance of one,'' he
called.

She hit the button to lower the passenger window
and tell him to forget it, but he'd disappeared into the
back of the ambulance before she had the chance.

As the ambulance pulled out of the driveway and
sped away, Callie realized that Gloria stood on the
lawn, holding the baby and curiously watching her.
''Are you dating Doc?''

''No! Absolutely not.''

A merry sparkle lit her coal-black eyes. ''He's never
charged *me* a fee like that.''

Callie's face grew warm. "He was being deliberately impertinent. You know what an incorrigible flirt he is."

"That's true," she agreed with a laugh.

Callie didn't think it was particularly funny. Feeling disgruntled for no good reason, she shoved the key into the ignition, then cast another glance at Gloria through the open passenger window. "I think you should know that I didn't come to the Point for social purposes. I'm investigating a lawsuit."

Gloria stepped closer, her face bright with curiosity. "Grant Tierney's lawsuit against Doc?"

Callie hadn't been sure the matter was common knowledge. She should have known better, in a community like Moccasin Point. "Actually, it's Agnes's lawsuit."

Gloria rolled her dark, expressive eyes. "Everyone knows it's Grant pushing to sue." She patted the baby on her shoulder and treated Callie to a friendly smile. "I'm glad you're investigating. Jack is too good a doctor to make a mistake like Grant is claiming. I hope you prove the claim is bogus."

Callie gazed at Gloria in dismay. She'd jumped to a very wrong conclusion—that Callie was working on Jack's behalf. "Gloria, I...I won't necessarily be trying to disprove the claim," she explained haltingly, hating to admit that she and her sister worked for the Tierneys. "I'm going to gather whatever evidence I can find, no matter whose side it proves or disproves."

"Of course. You've got to be objective. Any good investigator is, I'm sure. I'm just glad it's you investigating the case instead of someone in Grant Tierney's pocket."

Callie debated the wisdom of explaining anything more.

"Let me know if I can help you," Gloria offered. "I'm

sure everyone on the Point will want to help Doc all they can."

"Thank you." As much as Callie wanted to question her, she balked at the idea of doing so under false pretenses. Gloria was, after all, a personal friend.

"I was there at the picnic where it happened, you know."

"Did you see Jack give Agnes the injection?"

"No. I didn't even know that he had. But I was snapping photos of everyone all day."

"Photos?"

"I always take photos. A hobby of mine. I don't know if any of them will help with your investigation, but you never know. Would you like to see them?"

Callie pulled the car key from the ignition. Photos had too much potential to pass up. "Please."

Gloria spent over an hour with Callie, showing her photos she'd taken at the picnic, allowing her to look through others and giving her prints or negatives of any she chose.

One photo showed Jack lounging near a tree with a beer in his hand. Callie supposed it might prove to be damaging if the jury believed he'd been drinking before administering the injection. She'd have to ask around to determine if he *had* been.

Callie didn't feel her usual satisfaction at finding a promising angle. She felt reluctant to take the photo at all.

She forced herself to take it. Business was business.

Gloria also gave her photos of Jack at other picnics. In one, he sat on a huge, black motorcycle with an open leather vest hanging from his massive shoulders. He wore torn jeans. His jaw was shadowed by beard stubble, and his scar dominated one side of his face, much more intrusive than it appeared now. He looked more like a wild outlaw biker than a surgeon.

Another photo featured him bare chested on the beach with two bikini-clad women. One of his buddies had stuck a stethoscope around his neck, as Gloria laughingly explained. She'd written beneath the picture, "Doc Forrester, hard at work."

The photos, Callie knew, could be used to portray him in a decidedly unprofessional light—not the image his defense lawyer would like to project to a jury.

Gloria believed Callie wanted the photos for old-times' sake, since most of them featured her childhood friends. It wasn't until she had left Gloria's house and returned to the inn that Callie's conscience got the best of her.

What was happening to her? She was simply doing her job—looking for leads and gathering items that might prove useful. Why, then, did she feel so guilty?

Sitting near the phone in her suite at the inn, Callie imagined how Gloria would feel when she learned the truth. *Betrayed.* Hovering over the phone, Callie debated calling her and confessing her true role in the malpractice case.

It wouldn't be wise.

She had to tell her, though. Perhaps, if the truth came from her, it wouldn't seem like such a betrayal.

Taking a deep breath, she dialed the phone. Gloria's warm greeting only made the confession more difficult. Holding the phone tightly, Callie explained the circumstances she hadn't mentioned—that her sister Meg was representing Grant Tierney in the lawsuit, and that she herself had been hired by Meg.

"But you came to my house with Doc," Gloria said.

"I saw him kiss you. How can you be working against him?"

"I know it seems strange, but—"

"Does he know you're working against him?" she asked, her voice suddenly sharp with suspicion.

"Yes, of course he does. But he says he hasn't done anything wrong, so the investigation can't hurt him, and the truth will eventually speak for itself."

"That does sound like something he'd say," Gloria cautiously judged, as if trying to evaluate how much to believe.

"Gloria, do you want me to return the photos?" Callie half hoped she would. Though Meg would definitely want them, they weren't really evidence in the malpractice case itself.

"The photos?" Gloria repeated in alarmed surprise. "They can't be used to hurt Doc, can they?"

"I'm not sure," she hedged.

Gloria's silence bothered her far more than any reproach would have. After a long pause, Gloria quietly said, "Do whatever you feel is right. If you're planning to stab Doc in the back, you'll copy those photos before you return them to me, anyway. Personally, I'm betting that you won't use them."

Gloria hung up without a goodbye.

Callie felt worse than she had before she'd made the call. After a glum moment, she shook herself out of the doldrums. She'd been crazy to offer to give the photos back. She couldn't let personal issues like friendship interfere with her job.

Carefully she tucked the photos into her briefcase.

Determined to finish her business on the Point as quickly as possible, she called a couple of the witnesses on her list and obtained permission to drop by their

houses after supper. She set an appointment to inter-
rogate the hospital staff on Tuesday. She then drove
Jack's car to the county courthouse, where she spent
the remainder of the Friday afternoon searching the
records for previous lawsuits against him.

She couldn't help feeling relieved when her search
produced no previous lawsuits. Angry at herself for
that relief, she dined alone at a roadside café, then
drove to Sally Babcock's house to keep her first appointment of the evening.

Sally, it seemed, had been forewarned about her role
in the investigation. She greeted Callie with an unmis-
takable coolness, then told her about the wonderful
care Dr. Forrester had given her son after an accident;
how he'd delivered her grandbaby when they couldn't
get to the hospital in time; how he'd diagnosed a condition of hers before she'd known there was a problem.

One question Sally hadn't been prepared for: had
there been shrimp in her gumbo at the picnic?

Her answer had been a no. Which gave credence, of
course, to Grant's claim that Agnes's allergic reaction
had been imagined. This would mean that Jack's injection had been unnecessary, and opened the door to
speculation as to whether he'd administered the right
medication.

Bad news for Doc.

Callie wouldn't let it bother her. She slipped the tape
of the recorded conversation into her briefcase and
went on to the next witness's house, who had nothing
useful to tell her.

She returned to the bed-and-breakfast inn around
eight o'clock, wondering if Jack would be waiting for
her there.

He wasn't.

She felt both disappointed and relieved. As much as she'd warned him about her intention of gathering "dirt" to use against him, she wasn't looking forward to facing him after a day of doing just that. On the other hand, she wanted to reclaim her car and give him the key to his, putting an end to his reasons for contacting her.

That, of course, was the most important thing—putting an end to their personal contact.

Tossing her briefcase aside and kicking off her high-heeled shoes, she fell wearily across the canopied bed and thought about Jack's impending visit. She would greet him at the front door of the inn, exchange car keys and bid him a firm farewell. Maybe then her precarious emotional state would return to normal and she could do her job without all these bothersome qualms.

She certainly wouldn't pay his "unpaid balance" of a kiss. The very thought of it, though, sent blood rushing to her head. She knew he hadn't meant the quick, casual kind of kiss he'd given her at Gloria's. Oh, no...not Jack. He meant one of those long, hot, intricate kisses that had stirred her so deeply.

He knew it would lead to another. And another...

Callie closed her eyes, lounged against the bed pillows and savored the memory of his kisses. She'd never felt such intoxicating passion burn in her blood; passion that transformed her into a purely sensual being; passion that demanded she disregard everything and make love to him.

Exhaling a long, heated breath, she opened her eyes and stared at the ceiling, feeling overly warm and somewhat dizzy with sensual longing. She, the "queen of cool," who rarely dated a man long enough to become physically intimate, couldn't believe she was lying here, reliving a man's kisses. Wanting to taste his mouth again and incite the power of his muscled body.

She released her two-fisted grip of the bedspread, sat up and raked shaky fingers through her hair. She couldn't allow herself to think about Jack Forrester with such physical yearning.

He'd collected that last quick kiss without her approval or any regard for privacy. If she met him at the main entrance of the inn tonight, would he try the same? She'd be on her guard this time, and she'd set him straight. There could be nothing personal between them.

As she waited for his visit, she organized her notes and ironed her clothes, listening the entire time for the telephone. Ten o'clock came and went. She turned on the television and tried to watch it. Her attention continually strayed.

A fee of two kisses. How preposterous! And devious. Was he thinking about the "unpaid balance" even half as much she was?

Eleven o'clock ticked by.

Maybe another emergency had kept him later than he'd expected. Or maybe he'd found something else he'd rather do with his Friday night. She tried not to think about what that "something else" might entail.

With whom, she wondered, had he planned to catch a ride home? The hospital was an hour drive from the Point, with only wilderness, marshland and highway in between. Who would drive him all that way, late at night, after work? Knowing Jack, a beautiful young woman would. He was probably with her now.

He might be paying her a fee for the ride…in kisses. Not that Callie cared. She didn't!

She clicked off the television and paced across the room. He could spend all night, every night, with dozens of beautiful women, like the ones who posed in the beach photo with him. She merely wanted her car back, she sullenly told herself.

The clock struck midnight. Then half-past twelve.

She gritted her teeth. He'd promised to come to her this evening, and he'd broken that promise. It felt rather good to be angry with him; to resurrect the old feelings of being abandoned while he busied himself with other pursuits. She'd almost forgotten how unreliable the man could be.

Her growing anger at him lessened the confusion that had plagued her all evening. *Of course* she wanted nothing personal to do with him. *Of course* her career was more important than any sappy emotional concerns. *Of course* she'd never, ever, become sexually involved with Jack Forrester.

Tomorrow at the picnic, she'd interview everyone who could possibly further her case. She'd follow up on leads, keep her appointment Tuesday with the hospital staff, then head back to Tallahassee. No qualms, no regrets.

She bathed, brushed her teeth, changed into her camisole nightie and headed for bed. As she reached to draw down the bedcovers, a sudden noise stopped her. It sounded like something small and hard hitting the window.

The sound came again, and Callie moved toward the closed French doors that led to a private balcony. As she peered cautiously out into the moonlit darkness, a small, hard object struck the glass. A pebble.

She suddenly understood.

When they'd been kids, Jack had thrown pebbles at

her bedroom window late at night. She'd sneaked out of the house and they'd gone on nocturnal adventures—gigging flounders in the sand, gathering scallops on the spits, fishing off private piers.

In later years, he'd thrown pebbles at Meg's window. Callie had lain awake, listening to Meg sneak out of the house, wondering what adventures Jack and she would share. She'd doubted they would gig for flounders.

She'd been angry back then, she now realized with surprise. Angry and hurt that Jack had chosen Meg.

The realization seemed nothing short of a revelation. For so long, she'd believed her own version of the truth—that she was angry at Jack for *hurting* Meg. Although it was true, she realized now that she'd also been angry before then.

He'd been Callie's friend, and as they'd blossomed into teens, she'd wanted him to kiss her, to want her as more than a pal. He hadn't. He'd wanted her older, prettier sister.

The truth about her anger embarrassed Callie. No wonder she'd buried it beneath a more acceptable truth. More alarming was that, after all these years, she hadn't forgiven him.

Had he kissed Meg in the same passionate way that he'd kissed Callie today? Had he whispered nonsensical but stirring comments that had made her feel she was the only girl in the world for him? If so, she couldn't blame Meg for believing he would be there when she needed him.

He'd let her down, though, and moved on to the next girl.

Another pebble bounced off the window, jarring Callie solidly into the present.

Don't open those French doors, she warned herself, dazed by her own emotional reaction to a drama played out years ago. *Don't step out onto that balcony.* He'd come too late to conduct any civil form of business. The exchange of cars could take place in the morning.

A soft, birdlike whistle sounded through the September night. Another signal they'd used as kids, to clue each other in on a hiding place.

Callie bit the inside of her cheek and folded her arms around her bare shoulders and satiny camisole. She would *not* open those doors. Not in a million years.

She knew the business he'd come to conduct. He'd be asking her to pay that "unpaid balance." He'd be wanting to kiss her.

The warmth stirred low in her stomach.

Another signal reached her ears—the one he'd worked so hard to perfect. Though he'd meant it as an exotic birdcall, it had always sounded more like a wounded chimpanzee to Callie.

A reluctant smile pulled at her mouth. He'd have everyone at the inn peering over the balconies in alarm if he kept *that* up. Surely he had to realize it.

The chimpanzee call came again. Callie rolled her eyes. The man was shameless and brazen, and endlessly annoying.

She unlocked the French doors to tell him so.

6

"SHHHH! GO AWAY," Callie whispered, opening the doors only wide enough to stick her head through. "You'll have everyone running out here to see where the chimpanzee noises are coming from."

"Chimpanzee?" His soft, deep voice wafted from somewhere below the small, private balcony. "Now that's hitting below the belt. Don't you know a jungle bird when you hear one?"

She bit her lip to stifle a laugh. She certainly didn't want to encourage him. "Has anyone ever told you you're annoying?"

"Yeah. A friend of mine named Callie Marshall. Know her?"

An unexpected feeling of loss settled into her stomach. *I used to know her.* Needing to change the subject, she demanded, "How did you find out which room was mine?"

"I asked Dee's boys yesterday."

Callie rolled her eyes. "Go away, Jack."

"Come down, Cal. I brought your car."

"We can exchange cars in the morning."

"I'll need mine tonight, in case I'm called out on an emergency. And I'm sorry I got here so late. The only ride I could find was with old Walt, in hospital maintenance. His shift didn't end until eleven. Besides, I stopped to hose off your car after I hauled it out of the mud. Didn't think you'd want to drive it the way it was."

Gratitude, guilt and a host of emotions too jumbled to name drew her hesitantly onto the balcony where she searched the moonlit darkness below, feeling the need to at least make eye contact with him. She'd obviously wronged him with her suspicions earlier. He'd not only kept his promise, but he'd gone out of his way to help her even more than she'd expected, after a long shift at the hospital, yet. She leaned her forearms on the sturdy wooden rail. "Thank you for bringing my car. You didn't have to hose it off."

"I wanted to." He stepped back to where they could see each other more clearly.

Her heart missed a beat at the sight of him. He looked so tall and manly, his shoulders broad and strong, his stance wide legged, his face etched in shadows. His hair glinted the very color of moonlight, and his whisper took on an alluring gruffness in the summer-soft night. "We need to exchange car keys. Come down, Cal."

She swallowed, knowing he wanted more than just his key. She was terribly tempted. "You can toss my key up to me, and I'll drop yours down to you."

"It's too dark. It'll get lost in the grass."

"Then you'll have to wait until morning."

"I have a better idea."

She watched as he picked up a garden bench and carried it to somewhere below the balcony. "Are you going to stand on the bench for me to hand you the key?" Vague disappointment tempered her relief that the dilemma had been solved. "Jack?"

A moment went by. She heard a dull thud, a muffled

curse and a scrape that could be boots scuffling against the brick building.

"You're not trying to climb up here, are you?" she guessed, growing apprehensive. "You'd better not." A cry of dismay escaped her when his hands gripped the bottom of the balcony rail and the shaggy golden top of his head came into view.

"You're crazy," she whispered fiercely, hovering over him as he climbed. "Someone will see you and call the police. You'll fall and break your neck. You'll…oh, my…" Her heart thudded with anxiety as she backed away and he hoisted himself over the rail.

He settled solidly onto his booted feet beside her, then beamed a crooked smile. "Didn't think I could do it, did you?" His cocky satisfaction over the silly stunt brought back vivid memories.

She wanted to choke him for scaring her. "You could have stood on the bench and reached for the key. I would have handed it to you."

"Gee." He tilted his head and dazzled her with a breath-stealing smile. "I hadn't thought of that."

She almost snorted. "Do you realize how much trouble you'd be in right now if I called the police?"

He leaned negligently against the rail. Wearing a black T-shirt and tight black jeans, his gilded hair tousled around his ruggedly attractive face, he looked like her fantasy version of a cat burglar. "Go ahead. Report me."

"I might do that."

His amber gaze wandered in leisurely paths over her face and hair. She drank in the masculine beauty of his face, dappled in moonlight and shadow. The sweet, heady scent of lotus blossoms and wild Bermuda grass wafted to her on the sultry night breeze, intoxicating her a little. Frogs and crickets thrummed loud and steady, like the blood drumming in her ears. The sea, with its ageless song and tidal pull, filled her with an odd sense of destiny.

The smile gradually faded from his eyes as his gaze left her face and absorbed the rest of her.

She felt his warm perusal touch her everywhere, as bold and lingering as a caress. Crossing her arms over her breasts to stop the silent seduction, she wrapped her fingers around her bare upper arms. The satin camisole, barely covering the matching briefs, left her daringly exposed. The spaghetti straps had slipped from her shoulders, and other than a lacy trim around the panties' edges, her legs and thighs were entirely bare. No worse than a bathing suit, she told herself. Yet, the exposure stirred her blood with a heady sense of power.

His stare returned to hers with vital new heat. "When did you get so damn beautiful?"

Heat kindled beneath her skin. He virtually consumed her with his eyes, making her want to show him more. He affected her far too easily. "I'll get your key." She turned in subdued panic toward the French doors.

He shifted his powerful body to block her way, but it was his entreating gaze that stopped her. "First," he whispered, "I want to collect the rest of my fee."

Her breath hitched in her throat. "I don't know what fee you're referring to," she lied.

"A kiss." A smile lifted one end of his mouth, but his gaze remained hot and serious. "You owe me a kiss."

"I never agreed to that."

"You did." His fingers skimmed along the curve of her face, then sifted through her hair, infusing her with a desire to feel more of his touch. "Not with words, but with your eyes." His thumb caressed a slow, seductive path beside her mouth. "Kiss me, Callie," he breathed. "Please. I've been thinking about it all night."

Traitorous heat flushed through her. She wanted so badly to give in. But it wouldn't be just one kiss, and they both knew it. She had to force herself to remember the reasons she couldn't get intimately involved with him—the malpractice case, and her professional reputation.

And past betrayals.

She drew in a much-needed breath. "So…you think I'm beautiful now, Jack?"

He closed his eyes and brushed his mouth lightly across her lower lip. "God, yes."

"Because I have a few decent curves," she whispered, "and a fairly good haircut?"

As the words permeated the warm, sensual haze clouding his mind, Jack paused into stillness, then slowly drew back to study her face. The question gave him the feeling he wasn't on solid ground.

Not that he'd expected to be. She'd had a whole afternoon to talk herself out of kissing him again.

"If you're asking why I think you're beautiful," he slowly replied, sensing that only the God-honest truth would do, "I'd have to say that I'm basing my judgment on a purely personal gut reaction." His gaze pressed deeper into hers. "I've never seen a woman more beautiful," he swore in a heartfelt whisper.

Color bloomed in her cheeks, and she looked shaken.

He knew he had to lighten the moment. "Not that I don't appreciate a few decent curves and a good haircut."

She inhaled sharply through her nostrils and jerked

away from him. The peach satin of her wicked little night slip shimmered in the moonlight, pulling taut across her breasts and rising higher across her panties as she planted a hand on her hip. "Did you say the same kind of things to Meg?"

"Meg!"

"Shh!" Callie lunged to cover his mouth with her hand as the light on the balcony above them flicked on.

A murmur of voices sounded from directly above them. She warned him with widened gray-green eyes and urgent pressure at his mouth to stay silent.

Hooking his arm around her slim waist, he opened the French doors, swung her inside and closed the doors. Her hand had fallen from his mouth and settled against his shoulder. She remained in the crook of his arm, close enough for her breath to warm his neck and chin.

"Be very, very quiet," she whispered. "I don't want anyone to know you're here."

He nodded. She cautiously backed away from him.

He, personally, didn't give a damn who heard them, but he obligingly kept his voice low. "Now what the hell was your question about Meg?"

Her chin lifted, and the militant light flashed again in her eyes. "Did you tell her the same kind of things?"

"What kind of things?"

"You know." She hesitated, glanced briefly away and blushed. "That you thought she was the most beautiful woman you've ever seen."

"I didn't feel that way about Meg."

"Isn't that odd? She thought you did."

At a loss for words, he spread out his palms in a plea for enlightenment. "What are you trying to say, Callie?"

"You broke Meg's heart."

"I *what?*" He couldn't have been more stunned.

"You used her, then threw her away."

He sat down abruptly into the nearest chair, stared at her as he absorbed the impact of the accusation, then rubbed his hand over his eyes with a brief, silent laugh. "Used her," he repeated, lowering his hand to stare again at Callie. "And just how did I do that?"

Her glare was nothing less than lethal.

Jack's gaze narrowed. "Is that where you got all your hostility toward me?" He rose from the chair and stalked toward her. "From a delusional belief that I broke Meg's heart?"

"Don't sound so surprised." She boldly confronted him, both hands on her hips. "She's my sister, Jack. You know how you feel about Becky?"

"Yeah?"

"That's how I feel about Meg."

The magnitude of her anger finally hit home. Did she feel something similar to the sick, helpless rage that overcame him every time he thought about what Grant Tierney had done to Becky? He ground his teeth in frustration. He couldn't stand to have Callie think of him that way.

He gazed at her in solemn earnestness. "I swear to you, Callie, there was never anything serious between Meg and me."

"That's my point." A little catch in her voice refuted the coldness in her gaze. "You say there was nothing serious between you, but some women take things a lot more seriously than you do. Meg and I are two of those women."

Understanding then dawned in a sudden, clarifying rush. "You think I had sex with her, don't you?"

The question clearly caught her by surprise. "That's...that's none of my business."

"Did Meg say I had sex with her?"

"Of course not! Meg never told me things like that. I was her kid sister, for Pete's sake. But I'm not stupid. When a smooth-talking stud like you comes calling on a girl like Meg in the middle of the night, I doubt it's to gig flounders!"

"Smooth-talking stud," he repeated in quiet affront. Her cutting tone had made it very clear she hadn't meant it as a compliment. He tightened his mouth and loomed closer to confront her point-blank. "You think I lured Meg out of the house, plied her with flattery and persuaded her to have sex, don't you?"

"Well, didn't you?"

He stared at her for a full, tense moment, angry that she thought he'd do that. But then he recalled his hormonal teenage self and blew out an explosive breath. "I tried," he admitted with an embarrassed laugh. "I damn well tried." Not proud of that fact, he paced away from her and rubbed the back of his neck.

"Are you trying to tell me that Meg turned you down?" Callie scoffed, following him across the bedroom suite. "It won't wash, Jack. She was crazy enough about you to do anything."

"Yeah," he agreed with a nod, turning to face her. "I always liked that about Meg."

Callie's eyes glittered in warning.

"I liked her eyes, too," he mused, studying Callie's. "They were shaped a lot like yours, except they weren't green." He thought back, trying to picture them. "I don't remember what color they were, but I know they weren't green."

"Blue," Callie said, looking unsure of his point.

He wasn't entirely sure of his point, either. But he kept on, trusting he'd eventually arrive at it. "I also liked her voice. Soft, throaty, feminine. She sounded a lot like you...at least, when you're being nice." He nudged her stubbornly squared jaw with his thumb.

She cocked her face away from his touch.

He recaptured her gaze with the force of his stare, intent on explaining how he'd felt about Meg. He hadn't quite understood it himself until now. "I liked her mouth best of all, Cal." A flicker of hurt darkened her eyes, and he suddenly knew the point he'd been trying to make. "Do you know why?"

With a slight wince, she shook her head. "I don't think I need to know."

His voice degenerated into nothing more than a husky whisper. "Because it made me think of yours."

Dazed surprise replaced the hurt in her eyes.

His gaze returned helplessly to her mouth, so smooth, lush and ripe-peach red that he had to clench his jaw to stop from tasting it. "The only problem was," he went on gruffly, "kissing her wasn't the same as how I'd dreamed kissing you might be."

She drew in an audible breath and seemed to hold it.

"I never made love to her, Cal. We necked in the back seat of my car. Steamed up the windows. But when it came right down to it—" he shook his head "—I never went very far. Because I knew I wasn't being fair." His gaze burned into hers. "It wasn't Meg I was kissing."

If any sound disturbed the silence, it had to be the slow, heavy pounding of his heart. And maybe hers.

She sat down on the country sofa beside a quaint fireplace, folding her long, elegant legs beside her. "If you're trying to say you thought about *me*," she whispered, "I don't believe it. You barely noticed I was female."

"You seemed to prefer it that way." He paced slowly across the small living room area, his thumbs lodged in the front pockets of his jeans, his gaze fixed on her. "You chopped your hair off short enough that you never had to comb it. You'd die rather than wear a dress. You never tried makeup or jewelry. You lived in T-shirts, jeans and a scruffy old baseball cap." He stopped before her and gave in to a reminiscing laugh. "You cussed as bad as the boys. At least, when you were showing off. Your knees and elbows were always scraped up from sliding into base, climbing rocks or falling off dirt bikes. And when a guy made you mad enough, you'd slug him in the mouth."

"Yes, well…" She raised her chin but evaded his gaze, as if embarrassed by the charges but unable— and unwilling—to deny them. "That's what I mean. You saw me as one of the guys, so—"

"I didn't say that." He sat down beside her on the sofa and shifted his body to face her, virtually trapping her against the curved arm. His knee pressed against her bare, folded legs, and he felt their softness and warmth clear through the denim of his jeans. "There were times," he uttered, "when I just couldn't help noticing you weren't one of the guys."

She regarded him with an odd vulnerability. "Like when?"

He hesitated, finding it surprisingly hard to admit secrets he'd once struggled to hide from her. "Like when you'd eat an ice-cream cone."

"An ice-cream cone?"

Inwardly smiling at her bemused expression, he relaxed against the cushions and extended his arm along the sofa back, near the nape of her neck, immersing himself in her scent, her beauty, her nearness. "You had a way of savoring that ice cream that just made me…mmm…stare." A reminiscent warmth rolled into his chest. "At your mouth, mostly," he whispered. "Sometimes I'd picture it all damn night. And I'd think about kissing."

The color climbed into her face, as it always had when he'd stared at her. "Kissing…me?"

"Absolutely." Images of her from the distant past returned with earthy eroticism. She hadn't been pretty then, not by any stretch of the imagination, but she'd nearly driven him crazy. "I remember when you used to wear those cutoff jean shorts," he gruffly recalled. "They kept fraying with every wash, and by the end of the summer, they only came to here." He ran his fingers across her bare thighs, daringly close to the lace edges of her peach satin panties. Heat rippled through him at the intimacy of the contact, and the taut, silky feel of her skin, and the memory of how her slender thighs had affected him back then.

Her lips parted in clear response to his touch. Her breathing deepened, and in a throaty murmur, she inquired, "So then you didn't really mind my cutoffs?"

"Hell, no. I didn't mind those jeans that fit so tight, either." He vividly remembered the smooth, alluring curve of her hips, and their scintillating swing when she walked, even when she'd been so set on acting tough. Just thinking about her unwitting sexiness made him long to run his hands up and over her curvaceous hips, then around to the shapely back side of those little satin panties.

"My jeans were never that tight," she argued with a breathy little laugh.

"Then maybe I just liked what was in 'em."

Their gazes connected in a flash of heat.

"You hid it well," she whispered.

"I tried."

"Even the times I caught you staring at me, you ended up making wisecracks about the freckles on my nose or the braces on my teeth, and ran off to be with someone else."

He frowned at her take on his behavior. "I had to."

"Why?"

Because wanting you scared the hell out of me. Surprised by his own gut response, he glanced awkwardly away. "Damn, Callie, we were pals. Buddies. I felt like a jerk, thinking about you in that way." He paused, unable to explain how torn he'd felt. Instead, he tossed her a rueful grin. "I figured that if you knew, you'd slug me."

Not exactly a lie, but not really the truth. The main reason he'd kept a safe distance from her was a strong conviction that if he didn't, he'd be lost. Seriously lost. Caught under some crazy spell. Robbed of control.

Control had been important to him then, with his plans for college, med school and single-handedly saving the world's population. Now that he'd met some goals and modified others, control was still important—except he had more confidence. He'd learned how to maintain his control, no matter what.

He exerted some of it now to stop himself from coming on too strong. "I probably would have risked the slugging," he reflected as lightly as he could, "if you hadn't been so naive."

"Naive!" She gaped at him. "I wasn't naive."

"You were a babe in the woods, sweet and pure."

"Sweet and pure!" Astonishment sparkled in her gray-green eyes. Leaning casually against him, she cupped her hands to his ear. "Hello? Is Jack there?" He pulled away with a laugh. Her mouth twisted into a smirk. "The 'pure' part might have been technically true—*might* have been—" she stressed, "but the Jack Forrester I knew never thought I was sweet *or* pure."

He grinned, thoroughly enjoying the Callie Marshall he thought he'd lost forever. "The 'pure' part was definitely true. You'd probably never even been kissed before you left the Point."

She arched a charmingly coy brow. "You're laboring under a grave misconception."

He stared at her in disbelief. "Are you telling me some guy kissed you?"

She poked her tongue against her cheek and harbored her secrets.

His heart took a ridiculous dive. "Who?"

"None of your business."

"You didn't even date."

"As far as you knew."

He squared his jaw, feeling unreasonably pissed that some guy—whom he must have known—had been dating her on the sly. Behind his back.

Kissing her.

She smiled, looking a little too satisfied. Vindicated.

He laughed. "Yeah, well, despite all your vast experience, you were still naive. As green as they come."

"What makes you think that?"

"Little things." He tugged on a tendril of her thick, dark hair, savoring its silky texture and wildflower scent. "Like when I used to push you into the water. Did you know I did it on purpose?"

"Of course. You shoved me off docks, for Pete's sake."

"Did you know why?"

Looking doubtful that he'd had any ulterior motive, she searched his eyes. "For fun?"

"You could say that." His mouth quirked in a wicked grin. "You'd climb out of the water, all fired up and mad, charging at me, with your skin wet and glistening—" his voice caught "—and your thin cotton T-shirt clinging." He fell silent, stunned by the heat that coursed through him at the memory.

His gaze drifted irresistibly to her breasts. Rising and falling in a slow, hard rhythm beneath soft satin, they were somewhat more voluptuous now, but with the same jaunty, pointed nipples that had poked through the wet cotton. His stare returned to hers, his insides simmering. "You got me so hard, coming up out of the water like that, Callie," he whispered. "I'd have given anything to feel you."

Sensuality seeped like liquid heat into her gaze. "Know something?" she whispered. "I'd have let you."

His heart paused. His breathing suspended. *She'd have let him.* All those nights he'd lain awake wondering. Doubting. Finally he knew. He could have touched her. Kissed her. Maybe even loved her. But the knowledge itself wasn't nearly as momentous as the fact that she'd told him, here and now.

A provocative confession.

Why'd she tell him? His arousal pulsed to astonishing hardness at the possibilities. Did she mean she'd let him…*now?*

Regardless of why she'd said it, she'd opened an important door—not to the past, but to the woman she'd become. He had no idea where that door would lead.

It didn't matter. Wherever it led, he wanted to be there.

"Callie." His breath hadn't fully returned, and his voice emerged as a gravelly rasp. He didn't touch her. Wouldn't risk it. Couldn't bear for the door to close before he'd wedged himself inside. "Callie." He shut his eyes, needing her with too voracious a hunger. "I want that kiss now."

Electrified silence followed. His throat went dry and his pulse drummed as he waited for her response. He sensed movement beside him, as if she'd shifted forward to rise from the sofa. To walk away.

He sat locked in place, his eyes closed, as he braced himself for her rejection. He'd have to work damn hard this time to find a way to lighten the moment.

But then the womanly fragrance of her hair and skin filled his nostrils, and the inviting warmth of her body radiated from a stunningly close proximity.

And her slender forearms slid around his neck.

His blood warmed, his heart quickened. He opened his eyes.

Her face, luminescent in its beauty, filled his vision, just as her scent and warmth clouded his mind. "Before I pay you that kiss," she whispered, "I want to thank you for reminding me of all those times you pushed me in the water."

Her words crested over him like waves on the shore, ebbing and flowing while he concentrated on the sensual purr of her voice, the sulky swell of her lips and the understood promise of a kiss, all rendering him dizzy and hot and hard with desire.

She angled her mouth to within a sultry breath of his. He leaned in to facilitate the kiss, desperately longing to taste and feel and indulge.

She pulled back just far enough to dodge his mouth.

He frowned and met her gaze in confusion.

"I'll give you that kiss," she promised in a throaty murmur, "but only when I'm good and ready."

His confusion grew.

Tightening her arms around his neck, she pushed up higher on her knees, the satin of her camisole sliding against the coarse cotton of his shirt as she rose, until her head towered above his. "Until then, you'll have to be polite."

"Polite?" he managed to whisper, his attention again caught elsewhere. Her lush, hard-tipped, satin-clad breasts now hovered before him, eye level.

Mouth level.

Heat engulfed him.

"Don't even think about it, Jack." Her whispered command stopped him before he'd consciously realized he'd moved, and her elbows trapped his hands on their slide up her slender rib cage.

Frustration lurched in his gut. What the hell was she doing? Did she intend to kiss him, and hold him, and let him do all the things he wanted so damn much to do…or not?

With his muscles tensed, his arousal hard and his pulse pounding relentlessly, he lifted his eyes to hers and focused his attention entirely on her explanation.

"Before you make a move," she whispered, gazing down at him with heated sensuality and the slightest glint of mischief, "and I do mean *any* move, you'll have to say, 'Callie may I.'"

He stared at her, too stunned to think clearly, let alone reply.

"I might give you my permission." She tilted her head judiciously. "Then again—" her breasts brushed close enough for the body-heated satin to whisper across his face "—I might not."

7

SHE HADN'T PUT MUCH thought into her impulsive taunt. He'd pushed her into it, actually, with his provocative recollections and blood-stirring gazes and whispered confessions. *I never made love to her, Cal. It wasn't Meg I was kissing.*

He'd lifted a weight from her heart, and she suddenly felt light and free. He'd thrown pebbles at her window, and she'd come out to play. He'd empowered her.

That in itself was a turn-on. The balance of power between them had always seemed tipped his way. He'd been older, stronger, intrinsically virile. She'd been a renegade tomboy. He'd playfully lorded his mastery over her for too long.

She would lord over *him* now for the sheer fun of it. She'd go as far as her naughty whim would take her. She hadn't decided yet how far that would be.

Not very far at all, of course, if he couldn't bring himself to say "Callie may I."

With a heady rush of delight in her feminine power, she'd laid down the rules, thrown down the gauntlet. She'd virtually brushed her breasts across his face!

Warm tingles of physical reaction spiced the thrill of her own boldness. Her blood sang in her veins as she ran her hands over his mountain-hard shoulders and peered expectantly down at him. She anticipated at least a trace of a grudging smile.

He gave her no smile.

That fact gave her pause. She really had expected a smile.

Other than a subtle squaring of his jaw and a slight throb at his temple, he sat perfectly still, his muscled body rigid, his color high beneath his tan, his large hands gripping her sides where she'd trapped them.

His gaze, at first clearly stunned, left hers to pore over the breasts she'd thrust so near to his face. Her heart skittered and spun with sudden qualms as she watched from above, feeling her nipples tighten under the slow sweep of his visual exploration. He seemed so very serious. Perhaps she'd been too hasty.

"Callie." His eyes returned to hers with a hot, glazed intensity that set off alarms inside her. Hoarsely he whispered, "May I?"

Her knees went weak. Her heart fluttered in her throat. She supposed she should make him state his exact intentions, in keeping with the game—*her* game—but she squeezed out a barely audible "You may."

He exhaled a hard, torrid breath and slid his strong hands over the satin, up and down her rib cage, his thumbs brushing only the sensitive side swells of her breasts.

The feel of his hands on her and the intensity behind his caresses sparked flames in her blood, and he'd done little more than look her over.

"Callie." He brushed his face lightly against the side of one breast. "May I?"

Her heart tripped into double time, and through a thickening haze of sensuality, she tried to anticipate his next move. "You may."

Splaying his hands around her rib cage, he held her firmly captive and rubbed his face across her breasts, back and forth, slowly and deliberately. His beard stubble rasped against the satin, and his lips grazed her hardened nipples with every languorous turn of his head.

Callie reflexively arched, astounded by the keen pleasure shooting through her, and by the iron-strong tension in his hands, his arms, his body.

She sensed he held a savage power barely in check. She felt as if she'd taunted some powerful beast who now had her trapped between his paws.

The idea frightened her. Thrilled her.

He tipped her back, pressed her down against the curved arm of the sofa and relentlessly roused her nipples through the satin with his stubbled chin and firm, wide mouth. He kept his lips taut and parted just wide enough for his breath to steam in tingling paths, just wide enough for the sensitized peaks to catch between his lips and drag fleetingly across his tongue.

She whimpered and arched higher, pressing herself against his mouth, aching for hotter, longer contact.

He raised his head and stared at her with eyes of smoldering amber. "Callie..."

"You may, you may."

He swept the camisole down, out of his way, and filled his mouth with her breasts. Hot, swirling suction propelled her deeper into pleasure. Silky hair brushed across her jaw and throat. Lightning spears of sensation flashed to her innermost depths as he sucked and tugged on the pebble-hard tips.

She dug her fingers into his sinewy shoulders and held on tightly, feeling caught up in a gale-force storm of lusty pleasure. His hands pushed the crumpled camisole farther down her body, then coursed along her bare, heated skin from one curve to the next.

His mouth soon left her breasts and followed his hands with long, hot, savoring tastes.

"You may," she breathed, though he hadn't asked. She wove her fingers into his thick, golden hair as he passionately kissed, licked and swirled his way across her abdomen and down the curve of her hip. She writhed beneath his mouth and hands, adrift on a sea of heat and pleasure and restless need.

"Callie may I," he rasped, and before she'd recognized the words, he'd tugged her panties down. "Callie may I," he breathed, and brushed his mouth in a hot, lingering path above her curls.

Through an onslaught of sensations, she realized the profound intimacy of what he intended to do. Emotion gripped her heart with a tensile strength. She wanted this. Longed for this. Not only for the pleasure, but for *the intimacy.*

Panic flurried in her chest.

She gasped and reached for him with both hands, forcing his head up to meet her gaze. "I didn't give you permission," she whispered somewhat frantically.

His golden-dark brows converged, his hands tightened on her hips and wildfire leaped into his stare. Between ragged breaths, he forced out, "Callie may I."

She shook her head, giving way to the panic. She'd meant to play a game—a sexual game, yes—but somehow she'd forgotten how to win. She'd lost control, not of him, but of herself, and didn't know how to reassert it.

He expelled a forceful breath, then another, and for a moment, looked dangerously mutinous. But then he rose up onto a muscled forearm beside her, brushed her hair from her face and searched her eyes with tender, heated longing. "Are you good and ready to pay me that kiss now?"

That kiss. Lord, yes. Surely she could handle a simple kiss. She nodded, grateful for the relatively tame suggestion.

He angled his face across hers, paused, and invoked in a slow, lingering whisper, "Callie may I."

A moan escaped her as she met him in an irresistibly tender foray. He delved with moving thoroughness, leaving no room for reflection. Her panic soon ebbed, and before she knew it, the passion flowed again, carrying her in its wild currents.

Their kisses grew harder, deeper, more frenzied. They tumbled together from the sofa to the carpeted floor. He struggled out of his clothes, and she helped him, craving the feel of his skin against hers. The pleasure of that stunning, full-bodied connection pulsed through her like strong, hot emotion. He lulled her away from that thought with a particularly voluptuous kiss.

At sporadic intervals, he panted, "Callie may I."

She whispered just as randomly, "You may."

His hands flowed over her—kneading, caressing and molding her to his honed, muscled nakedness. An astonishing column of hardness burrowed against her abdomen. She couldn't help undulating her hips in an instinctive desire to slide it firmly into place.

Groans vibrated in his throat. Fever burned in his skin. His fingers surged between her legs, through the hot, damp curls, into her intimate heat.

She sucked in an audible breath. Her hips bucked. He wedged his knee between her thighs to part them farther, and then persisted, his fingers gliding, stirring and probing until fire danced in her loins, stoking her into a swelter of need.

She'd never felt such a mindless compulsion to draw a man inside her. Never wanted to make love as desperately as she wanted him now. The sheer intensity of her desire alarmed her.

She broke her mouth away from his kiss with a panicked gasp. "I...I didn't say you could." Urgently she sought his eyes, needing the connection. "You didn't—"

"It's okay, Cal," he gruffly interjected, his sweat-beaded face dark and intense above her, his gaze hot with persuasive emotion. "Don't be afraid. It's only me."

Only me. Only Jack. He'd meant to reassure her, she knew. He'd meant that he'd known her forever, and that he'd never hurt her, and that she risked nothing at all by making love to him.

None of those things reassured her. They only scared her more. But she didn't stop his large, hard, blunt-tipped fingers from their swirling invasion. She didn't slow her hips in their compulsive undulations.

Her eyes closed, her lips parted. A groan of helpless pleasure rolled from her throat. He wedged his fingers in deeper and pumped in a languid, maddening rhythm. His thumb worked the outside, catching her in an awesome pull. The most incredible pleasure built and spread, until she climaxed in great, shuddering contractions. Her thighs squeezed together, trapping his wrist between them. Her shoulders curled up off the floor. He caught her against his chest and held her as she quivered and quaked and fought for breath. Slowly, then, he inched his embedded fingers from her, sending renewed contractions through her loins.

Before those contractions had fully ended, he rolled her out beneath him, captured her mouth with another tumultuous kiss, and pushed himself slowly, deeply, into her.

She cried out and arched against him as his throbbing hardness filled her, stretching her to capacity. A whimper rose in her throat, and in an instinctive move to adjust to his size, she wrapped her legs around his lean, powerful hips.

And he began to move in slow, subtle thrusts and gyrations. Pleasure radiated through her core like molten heat.

A knock sounded at the door.

A loud, urgent, intrusive knock. "Ms. Marshall?"

Callie stiffened; Jack paused. They stared at each other in sweaty, panting confusion.

The knock came again. "Callie?" She recognized the feminine voice as Dee's, the innkeeper. "Are you in there, honey?"

"Y-yes," she stammered.

Jack closed his eyes briefly and rocked into her again. She drew a quick, reactive breath and met his heated gaze.

"Sorry to disturb you in the middle of the night like this, but we had a call from the people in the room beneath yours."

Callie strained through the sensual fog surrounding her brain to understand what the woman was saying. Jack had tightened his hold on her and thrust deeply into her again.

Her mouth opened in involuntary response.

The innkeeper outside her door rambled on, "They thought they saw someone climbing up onto your balcony. My husband's not home, so I called the sheriff."

"Tell her it was me," Jack rasped in a hot whisper against Callie's ear. "She'll go away."

She widened her eyes and shook her head as the ramifications of the situation sank in. She couldn't tell anyone she had Jack in her room! The news would spread across the Point by morning! "I...I didn't see anyone," she called, her voice weak and unsteady.

Jack cursed beneath his breath, his rugged face glistening with sweat. "Tell her, Cal," he insisted with gruff desperation.

She arched into another of his forceful thrusts. When she could speak again, she whispered, "I can't, I can't! No one can know you're here with me."

"Ms. Callie, this is Sheriff Gallagher," said another voice from the hallway.

Panic stirred in Callie's breast. Jack forced himself into stillness, shut his eyes and groaned. "Shh!" she said into his ear. "Be quiet, or they'll hear you."

"Good. They'll go away."

"I don't mean to scare you, ma'am," continued the sheriff, "but I found a bench pushed up against the house, directly below your balcony. I shone my light up there and didn't see anyone, but I'm concerned that the prowler might be hiding in one of those little alcoves on the sides."

"I'm sure he isn't," Callie assured him in a pitifully shaky voice.

"Prob'ly not. I'll bet it was just kids, playing around. We don't have much crime on the Point. But I can't take a chance with your safety, ma'am, or anyone else's. If you wouldn't mind, I'd like to take a quick look at that balcony myself."

"You mean you...you want to come *in?*"

"Yes, ma'am. Won't take but a minute."

"Get up, Jack!" she frantically whispered, wriggling her hips and twisting her body to disengage herself from him.

"God, Callie, don't do this to me." He grabbed for her hips to stop her from pulling away, but he was too late; she'd squirmed free. "Damn it, Cal, let me tell him I'm here, and explain why I—"

"Don't you dare!"

The sheriff cut into their whispered, wild-eyed confrontation. "Is everything okay in there, Ms. Callie?"

"Yes, yes, everything's fine," she cried. "Just give me a minute to...to find my robe. You...you woke me from a sound sleep."

"Sorry about that, ma'am. Just take your time."

Her panic grew as she thought about how Meg and Grant Tierney would take the news that she'd been caught with Jack Forrester in her room late at night. Pushing at Jack's chest, she rolled to her knees and scrambled to her feet.

Jack remained on the floor, half kneeling, half sitting, his erection huge and glistening, his eyes tightly shut, his jaw clenched.

She yanked at his muscled arm. "Get up, get up. You've got to hide."

He shot her a disbelieving glare. "Hide?"

"In the bathroom. No, no, someone might have to use it. Then what would I say? The closet. Hide in the closet."

"Hell, no, I'm not hiding in a closet."

Desperation forced her back down to her knees, where she gazed at him imploringly. "Please, Jack, please!"

Their gazes locked and shifted, while the sheriff

called out in a voice suddenly gruff with suspicion, "Ms. Callie, is someone in there with you?"

"No! No, of course not."

After a tense, reflective pause, the sheriff drawled, "Just in case that prowler's holding you at gunpoint or some such thing, I want you to tell me your daddy's first name. Give me the right one, and I'll know you're fine. Say the wrong one, and I'll have every man on the Point surrounding this building before the bastard can make a break for it."

Callie's eyes widened. Jack rolled his.

"My daddy's first name?" She choked, her throat suddenly tight with panic. At the vision of every man on the Point invading her room in the next couple moments, her mind had clouded over and she couldn't think of any name but "Colonel."

"Henry," Jack whispered.

"Henry!" Callie yelled out.

"Henry," repeated the sheriff. "Yeah, that's right. Henry." He sounded somewhat disappointed.

"There's no one in here with me, Sheriff," Callie emphatically assured him. "You probably hear the television. I fell asleep with it on. I'll turn it off, as soon as I find my robe." Frantically she tugged and pulled at Jack's arm until he grudgingly rose and allowed her to push him toward the closet.

"For God's sake, Callie," Jack whispered, "at least give me my clothes."

"Oh my God...your clothes!" She whipped around and searched the room wildly until she'd found his jeans, shirt and underwear. Piling it all into his arms, she yanked open the closet door and motioned him inside.

"If the sheriff opens this door," Jack grumbled, "he

and Dee will both go into cardiac arrest. Then won't I look cute, trying to tend to 'em buck naked."

"Shh!"

Tight-lipped, grim-faced and as splendidly naked as a Greek god, he held his wad of clothes beneath one muscled arm and allowed her to shut the door in his face.

With her heart thudding, Callie snatched her bath-robe from an armchair, shrugged into it and hurried to the door. By the time she greeted the sheriff and the stout, motherly blonde in a flannel bathrobe, Callie was out of breath and flushed with heat. "Come in, come in. Sorry I took so long. I—"

"Calm down now, Ms. Callie." The sheriff patted her arm as he strolled past her and into the suite. "I know I gave you a fright, waking you from a dead sleep and carrying on about a prowler, but you're safe now."

Dee followed him in, gazing at Callie in concern. "I'm so sorry about this. We've never had a problem with prowlers before, I swear. My husband will be home from his shrimping trip tomorrow, and he'll put an extra dead bolt on all the doors."

"Oh, Dee, I don't think that will be necessary," Callie said, watching the sheriff with a good deal of guilt as he stealthily approached the French doors, flashlight in one hand and a gun in the other.

"You ladies had better stand back, just in case."

Callie bit her lip as Dee grabbed her hand and held it tightly in both of her own.

"These doors aren't locked," the sheriff noted in a voice of stern disapproval. The squat, ruddy-faced lawman then flattened his back against one French door, pushed open the other and shone his flashlight out into the darkness. After a cautious pause, he ventured farther out.

Dee's grip on Callie's hand had grown painfully tight as she watched the sheriff with wide, anxious eyes.

Moments later, he stepped back into the room, closed the French doors and securely locked them. "No one out there now. It was probably just kids up to some prank."

Dee let out a dramatic sigh of relief and released her death grip on Callie's hand. "Better keep your room locked, Ms. Callie," advised the sheriff as he returned his gun to his holster. "You've got a lot of folks riled up over your investigation against Doc Forrester. I'm not saying anyone would do you harm, or even wish it, but they don't take kindly to anyone messing with one of their own."

One of their own. A pang of hurt went through Callie. She used to be "one of their own," too. But that had been too many years ago to count for much now.

"Folks are fairly used to putting up with Grant Tierney. They do it mostly for Agnes's sake, and because he's been buying up so much land around here," the sheriff continued. "But the doc is a great favorite. Never know what some people might do if they hear you're nosing around for something to use against him."

"Thank you for the advice, Sheriff," Callie said in a rather cool tone. She heard rustling in the closet, and said with renewed urgency, "I'm sure you and Dee can't wait to get back to your beds, just like I can't wait to get back to mine."

She'd meant it as a hint to hurry them on their way.

Instead, they both glanced toward her bed. Looks of mild surprise formed on their faces.

Too late, Callie realized that the bedding remained neatly made. No one could possibly have been sleeping in it. She felt warm color wash into her cheeks. "I, uh, fell asleep on the sofa," she mumbled in answer to their unasked question.

They then glanced at the sofa. Her peach satin camisole hung haphazardly from one cushion, and her lace-edged panties lay sprawled on the floor beside it.

The warmth in Callie's face deepened, but she offered no explanation. She could fling her panties and camisole wildly around the room if she wanted, couldn't she?

She then noticed Jack's boots lying on the floor beside the sofa, partially concealed in a shadow. Her heart turned over, and she shot a quick glance at both Dee and the sheriff.

Neither seemed to have noticed the boots, though. "If you see someone moving around the yard tonight, don't worry," the sheriff told her, reaching for the doorknob. "I'll be patrolling the grounds in case the intruder comes back."

Patrolling the grounds. Callie froze in dismay near the door as Dee and the sheriff shuffled past her into the hallway. How could Jack leave the inn undetected with the sheriff patrolling the grounds? And if Jack stayed until morning, Dee or her boys would surely see him leave. The entire population of the Point, including Grant Tierney, would know that Jack Forrester had spent the night in her room!

"Uh, Sheriff, I don't think it's necessary for you to waste your time patrolling the grounds. I was outside earlier, and I...I might have made some noise. That's probably what my downstairs neighbors heard.''

The sheriff frowned doubtfully. ''They reported the disturbance pretty late. About what time were you down there?''

''A little after midnight, I guess.''

''What were you doing down there after midnight?'' he asked, sounding genuinely curious.

''What was I doing?'' She cleared her throat. ''I was...looking at the stars. There's no place like the Point for stargazing, you know.''

''Isn't that the truth?'' agreed Dee. ''I didn't see many stars out tonight, though. Too cloudy.''

Callie clenched her hands so hard her nails dug into her palms. ''Yes. It really was a challenge to find them.''

The sheriff frowned in deep reflection then shook his head. ''Couldn't have been you the folks downstairs heard. Must have happened after you went in. Someone had to push that bench against the house. It didn't walk off the patio by itself.''

''The bench?'' She'd forgotten about the blasted bench! ''Oh, you mean the patio bench, against the house.'' She forced a laugh as she desperately searched her mind for an explanation. ''I moved it there.''

The sheriff blinked. ''*You* moved it there? Why?''

''Well, I spent so much time searching the sky for stars that my, uh...back started to hurt. My back goes out sometimes, you see, and I need a hard surface to lean against. So I—''

A choking noise, like someone losing the fight to hold back a laugh, ripped from the direction of the closet.

Callie raised her voice to mask it. ''So I pushed the

bench against the house and sat there. I just forgot to return it to the patio. I'm sorry. If I hadn't been sleeping so soundly when you woke me, I probably would have put it all together sooner. It's just a big misunderstanding, and there's no need for you to patrol the grounds, Sheriff, so please, please, *go home.*"

"I'm so relieved to hear that it was you, Callie," Dee cried. "I couldn't believe that we had a prowler."

"I guess I'm glad to hear it, too," the sheriff muttered rather crossly. "Feel like a damn fool, though, pulling out my gun and searching the balcony like some TV cop."

"No, no, I'm very grateful," Callie assured him. "You could have saved our lives. And your strategy in asking for my father's name—well, that was brilliant."

Another choking noise came from the closet, but Dee's enthusiastic agreement overrode it. Looking somewhat mollified, the sheriff followed the innkeeper down the stairs.

Callie shut the door, leaned against it and breathed out a long, tremulous sigh of relief.

The closet creaked open and Jack stepped out. He was wearing his black jeans, though he'd left them unfastened at his lean waist, and his shirt was slung negligently over one bare, broad shoulder. A smile curved his mouth and sparkled in his amber eyes as he sauntered toward her, furry chested, brawny and sinfully handsome.

"Oh my, Ms. Callie," he murmured as he approached, his warm gaze playing over her face and hair and short, black velour robe. "Better lie down on the bed and let me massage your back, seeing how all that aggressive stargazing threw it out."

"That's not funny."

"Oh, I agree." He leaned a hand against the door, just above her head, and angled his face intimately toward hers. "A problem like that can keep you flat on your back for quite some time. Good thing I have the next couple days off to doctor you through the, uh, *hard* times." He swept his hand in a lingering caress down her face. "And there's bound to be plenty of those."

The gathering heat in his gaze, the huskiness of his voice, the musky, masculine scent of his skin all conspired to keep her breathless and achingly aware of how intimate they'd become in the past hour.

What had she been thinking? She hadn't been thinking at all! She'd been mindlessly responding—to him, his charm, and the potent sensuality that sizzled through her blood whenever he touched her.

"You have to leave," she whispered, preparing herself to pull away. But then he slid his fingers into her hair and stroked her face with his thumb, diluting her willpower by alarming degrees.

"I don't have to leave," he countered in a gruff whisper. "I've got all night, and all day, and all night..."

"Jack," she groaned as he kissed the side of her throat, sending heat waves rushing through her. "This was a mistake." She caught his face between her hands, thrilling to the hot, abrasive feel of his jaw, remembering the rasp of it against her nipples. "It was my fault, I know. I shouldn't have taunted you like I did, with that silly game."

"You can make it up to me." He slid his hands around her waist, then up and down her velour-clad body. "We'll play my game now," he whispered against her mouth. "It's called, 'Please, Jack, please... make love to me.'"

He distracted her from her protest with a long, coaxing kiss. Her arms reflexively went around his neck. His hands caught at the robe's sash and tugged it free.

With a tortured groan, she came to her senses, pulled away from him and bunched the front of her robe with both fists to keep it closed. "I can't make love to you anymore," she cried, breathing heavily.

His brows knit in a protesting frown. "Why not?"

"It isn't right!" *And wanting you this much scares the hell out of me.* "I'm investigating a case against you, Jack."

"And you just now thought of that?"

"Yes." Misery sluiced through her as she belted her robe and backed away from him. She'd been unfair—taunting him, taking the game as far as she had, then stopping. "I'm sorry. I got carried away by all that talk about when we were young, and how you'd wanted me." She looked away from the heart-stopping intensity of his gaze and raked a trembling hand through her hair. "But we're not kids anymore, and I can't risk compromising the case, or the integrity of my firm, or my professional reputation by carrying on with the target of my investigation."

He crossed his arms and leaned a shoulder against the doorjamb in an eloquently insolent pose. "I don't see how making love to me can do any of that."

"I'm working for an attorney, who also happens to be my sister." She paced to a safer distance away from him. "Ethical considerations get very complicated, and if Grant Tierney felt his lawyer's team had conspired against him in any way—" She abruptly cut off her explanation.

Again she'd acted without thinking. She shouldn't be discussing these concerns with him. She picked up his soft leather boots from beside the sofa and handed them to him. "Get dressed. Please."

"We'll keep our relationship private, Callie." He obstinately tossed the boots down onto the carpet. "It's no one else's business. But even if someone does find out, they'll probably assume you're acting in the best interest of your client. You know, trying to pry information out of me."

She turned an affronted gaze to him. "Is that what you think I was trying to do—pry information out of you?"

"Of course not. The only reason I mentioned it is that a few of my well-meaning friends warned me against trusting you too much. They heard you were driving my car around today, and I guess Gloria saw me kiss you, so—"

"So now everyone thinks I'm seducing you to get information?"

"I don't think *seducing* is quite the right word. I mean, anyone in their right mind couldn't possibly imagine I'd resist."

"I wasn't the one who stood beneath this balcony and made chimpanzee calls!" she heatedly reminded him.

He winced. "Not chimpanzee."

"Are *you* trying to pry information out *me?*"

"Have I asked you any questions at all about the case?"

"Not yet."

"And I won't, either. I don't need to pry information out of you. I had people calling me at the hospital all evening, telling me about the photos you took from Gloria, the conversations you recorded, the court records you checked and the gumbo that didn't have shrimp in it."

Her jaw involuntarily lowered. "You knew about all that, and you still came over here?"

He ambled toward her, his golden-brown gaze warm and intent. "None of that has anything to do with you and me."

"Yes, it does," she replied with a catch in her voice, backing away. How could she reprimand him for coming here tonight when she had done so much worse? She'd gathered weapons to use against him, then taunted him into making love to her.

And now she was discussing her concerns for her professional reputation, when she'd come to Moccasin Point with the express purpose of destroying *his!*

She'd never been as confused in her life, and her chest felt ready to burst with contrary emotions. "Get dressed. You've got to leave."

"No one has to know I'm here, Callie, or that I've ever been here."

"Everyone will know! Your car is here, and so is mine. Someone is bound to notice that, and realize that you've been somewhere nearby…like, in my room! I'm surprised the sheriff hasn't already noticed."

"I've parked your car in the back garage and closed the door. No one will notice it's there. If anyone asks in the morning about when we switched cars, just say you left my key in my car, and you're not sure when I took it."

"You make it sound so reasonable, but I'm the one who would be hurt if the secret leaks out. What do *you* have to lose?"

"You."

The heated earnestness in his stare confused her all

the more. Her heart revelled in that heat, in that earnestness, while her rapidly declining reason warned her to run the other way. He wanted her now, but sex was only sex, unless she allowed herself to believe it was more.

And she wanted to believe it was more. She wanted to believe he felt something deeper for her than lust. Something stronger and finer and lasting.

The panic she'd felt while they'd been making love clawed at her once again. She'd spent twelve long years building up her defenses so she'd never emotionally need a man in her life again. She couldn't let those vital defenses melt away in the heat of Jack Forrester's lovemaking!

She turned blindly away from him, ready to snatch his boots up, thrust them in his arms and push him out of her suite.

Before she'd taken a full step, he caught her by the shoulders. "What are you afraid of, Callie? Don't tell me it has anything to do with your professional reputation. You weren't thinking about that while we were naked on the floor."

Her heart stood still. She couldn't argue with that.

"You panicked when things got too hot," he charged. "Why?"

"The...the sheriff was beating on the door," she hedged.

He shook her slightly. "Before that."

She stared at him in dismay. Of course he'd realized she'd panicked. *Don't be afraid*, he'd told her. *It's only me.* An ironic reassurance, since he was the only one who frightened her this way, the only one with the power to lay her heart dangerously open.

She swallowed hard and blinked away a sheen blurring her vision. He was wearing her defenses down too thin! "Go home, Jack," she begged.

His hands tightened on her shoulders. "I can't leave now, or someone will see me. We have to give Dee and everyone else time to go to sleep after the prowler scare. For all we know, the sheriff could still be out there."

Callie swallowed a groan. He was right. But how could she risk letting him stay for even a moment longer?

She felt too vulnerable now, with the virile scent of his heated body filling her head, and his hands squeezing her shoulders in a restless, needful way. Worse, though, was her inclination to read profound emotions into the sexual intensity radiating from him.

"Our best chance is if I leave just before dawn."

Which would give them another few hours.

She recognized the implacable set of his jaw and shoulders. He'd made up his mind to stay. The sheer familiarity of his willfulness touched her with traitorous affection.

How she missed her wild comrade at arms, and the rough-and-tumble girl she'd been, and the easy friendship they'd taken so for granted.

She forced through a tightened throat, "I'm sorry, Jack, for leading you on like I did. I'm so sorry! I never should have kissed you in the first place. I never should have gotten—" her voice broke into a whisper "—intimate with you."

"God, Cal, don't cry!" Looking shaken and troubled, he pulled her into his arms while she staunchly resisted tears of guilt and emotional confusion. "It's okay," he breathed against her hair. "Believe me, I understand. Nothing you've done has hurt me in any way." He rocked her in a tight, warm, bearlike hug that profoundly comforted her.

After a while, though, his rocking slowed into stillness and she became breathlessly aware of her face pressed against his bare, muscled shoulder, her torso molded to his and their heartbeats thundering through the thin fabric of her robe.

"The only problem is," he said in a hot, torrential whisper against her ear, "you *have* gotten intimate with me. It's too late to change that." He drew back and held her face between his palms. "So how could another few hours hurt?"

The ardent heat in his stare blazed straight through to her heart, trapping the air in her lungs and rekindling a need deep within her. "Come to bed with me, Callie," he hoarsely pleaded. "I won't do anything you don't want me to do, I swear."

She couldn't, at the moment, think of anything she didn't want him to do. In fact, when he gazed at her that way, she fiercely wanted everything.

"Only for tonight," she conceded in a wavery whisper, "and then never again. Never, ever, ever…"

He hushed her with a deep, hot, melting kiss.

8

HE'D LEFT HER, AS PROMISED, before dawn.

She'd been so physically and emotionally exhausted that she barely recalled his leaving. She'd fallen asleep with his strong body curved around her. When his warmth had separated from her, she'd reached through the darkness to pull him back.

He'd kissed her and whispered something soothing. Then he'd asked where to find his car key, and she'd mumbled, "Purse."

She'd fallen back to sleep missing him.

In the clear light of day, the stupidity of it all boggled her mind and kept her tense through breakfast in Dee's quaint dining room with other guests at the inn.

No one mentioned last night's prowler scare or Jack Forrester leaving the inn shortly before dawn. Callie assumed he hadn't been noticed. Thank God! If he'd been caught, word would have spread this morning like wildfire, and she would have dreaded this afternoon's picnic more than she was right now.

He would be there. Today. At the Labor Day picnic.

Apprehension flooded her. How would he act toward her with the community watching? How would she react to him? Could she look at him without outwardly responding to the incredible intimacies they'd shared last night? He'd made love to her in so many ways—with his mouth, his hands, his body. Every time, her climax had taken her somewhere new and wonderful. Every time, her emotional response had deepened.

Had their lovemaking meant anything to him other than a good time?

She almost choked over her coffee at the question. Of course not! It hadn't meant anything more to her, either, and she was glad of it. Damn glad.

Jack probably had more women to choose from than a sultan's harem. He'd probably pursued her for the simple novelty of it. Or the challenge, considering their history together. Or to influence her investigation.

All of those possibilities hurt too much to contemplate.

Without finishing her breakfast, she set her fork and napkin aside, snatched up her briefcase and hurried out to the parking lot. She would stick to her agenda: meet with Agnes this morning, talk to others at the picnic this afternoon, then lock herself in her room with a good book until her interview with the hospital staff on Tuesday.

Then she'd get the hell back to Tallahassee. She could handle the rest of the investigation from there—reports to write, doctors to consult, computer checks to run.

And she wouldn't, not once, think of Jack Forrester in a personal manner or worry about the impact her investigation might have on his career.

The sight of her sister's beige, mud-free Mercedes parked in the garage brought her up short. He'd towed the car out of the mud in the middle of the night and hosed it off for her. Then he'd tossed pebbles at her bedroom window, climbed up onto her balcony and made sweet, hot love to her until dawn.

She unlocked the driver's door, slid in behind the wheel and wilted against the leather seat. How could she possibly carry on as if last night hadn't happened? Whether she liked it or not, he had touched her deeply. He'd incited a powerful need within her that hadn't entirely subsided. And he'd made her remember how much she'd always cared about him.

She'd always cared. Deeply.

As a friend, she told herself. Nothing more than a friend.

Even so, she'd been fooling herself to think that she could run this investigation impartially. But if she didn't follow through with this case in an ethical, professional manner, how could she face herself, her employees, Meg, Grant or the Tallahassee business community?

After a long, inwardly chaotic moment, Callie reached a compromise: she'd search for the truth and nothing but the truth. She'd call Meg with that decision tonight. If Meg didn't like it, she could replace her with another investigator. Either way, Callie would gather no fuel for innuendo to sully Jack's name or prejudice a jury. She'd hand Meg no weapons to use against him, unless the truth itself turned out to be a weapon. If that proved to be the case, he'd brought the problems on himself.

She could live with that. Couldn't she?

"I HOPE OUR NEIGHBORS won't be as rude to you as they've been to me. Sally Babcock called to say she didn't appreciate having to answer questions about her gumbo." Agnes Tierney tightened her mauve-painted lips in indignation as she chopped olives at her kitchen work island. "And at Mr. Johnson's vegetable stand, Wanda Scaggs told me I should be ashamed for saying ugly things about Doc Forrester. Then Mr. Johnson himself snubbed me cold."

"Are you sure you want to go to the picnic today, Agnes?" asked Callie, watching the celebrated sculptress sprinkle the olives into a large bowl of Middle Eastern potato salad.

"Dear me, yes! Bob will be there. And my bridge club. They know this lawsuit is Grant's doing." She leaned over the bowl of salad to confide, "I believe this lawsuit is important to Grant because of a real estate deal. He's out with an agent right now, trying to set up the purchase of property near the end of the Point. He wants to build high-rise rental condos."

Callie stared at her in dismay. Unspoiled wilderness stretched for fifty miles in all directions from their small, Gulf Coast peninsula. Only a few dozen homes shared the lush landscape and pristine beaches. She hated to think of rental condos here and the development that would follow. "What does the real estate deal have to do with the lawsuit?"

"Jack owns the most important piece of land—the beach property. Without it, Grant can't swing the deal." Agnes's bracelets jangled on her wrist as she mashed garlic through a press. "I believe Grant wants to force him into selling."

Callie struggled to suppress her outrage. So Grant had more of a motive to exploit the situation than merely an adversarial relationship with Jack. He intended to use the unfortunate series of events to force Jack into a business deal. "Agnes, if you don't want to sue Jack, why are you?"

"I can't defy Grant!" she exclaimed with an anxious stare. "He hates to be crossed."

Callie bit her lip to stop from uttering advice that might prove unwise. From what she'd learned about Grant, he probably *would* cause Agnes too many problems if she defied him. Now more than ever, she wanted to get to the bottom of Agnes's mysterious malady last July. "Do you believe that Jack's injection caused your hallucinations?"

The willowy redheaded sculptress shrugged and poured lemon juice into the potato salad. "I suppose so. I'd never had hallucinations before, and haven't had them since."

"If the injection hadn't caused them, would you want to know what had?"

"Of course. I'd never falsely accuse a neighbor." She raised her slightly jowled chin, which set her dangling amethyst earrings into motion. "Not even Grant can stop me from apologizing if I've been wrong."

Remembering Grant's attempts to divert Agnes from prattling on about his ex-wives, Callie believed her. "Do you mind if I try to rule out other factors that might have caused them?"

"Oh, please do!" With a nervous glance at the doorway, she cautioned, "But if Grant comes home, you'll have to be discreet. He won't like you snooping around."

Callie spent the next hour questioning Agnes about her activities on that July day. Callie then took samples of the plants in the herb garden—from which Agnes had made herbal tea—and catalogued her stock of exotic spices. She even copied down the names of medication in the bathroom cabinet.

When she'd gathered all she could, she plugged her laptop's modem into a phone jack and sent the data to her assistant. She would send the herb and spice samples to the lab for analysis.

"I hope I haven't made you think poorly of Grant," Agnes said, removing the bibbed, red-and-purple print apron that had been protecting her long, dandelion-yellow kimono. "He's basically a good person." She tossed the apron aside and sat down at the table with Callie. "He just needs a wife who won't be afraid to stand up to him. That's why I think you'd be perfect. You have an aura of strength about you."

"Thanks, but I'm not in the market for a husband."

"Your feelings aren't hurt that Grant hasn't asked you to go to the picnic with him, are they? He's been too busy with this real estate deal to think about much else. I doubt if he'd go to the picnic at all if it weren't for the neighbors he wants to speak with. He has his eye on their land, too. So many projects in the works! He's hugely successful in business," she said with a touch of pride. "He'd make a fine husband for you."

Callie firmly guided the subject back to the July picnic. "If there was no shrimp in Sally's gumbo, why do you suppose you had an allergic reaction?"

"If the shrimp wasn't in the gumbo, it had to be in something else. I tasted shrimp."

Callie asked her to recall every dish she'd sampled.

After compiling a list, she slipped her notes into her briefcase and rose to leave. "Until we know what caused your reaction, you'd better be careful about what you eat at today's picnic."

"I'll only eat the food I bring," Agnes assured her. "Grant probably won't come to the picnic until later, but would you like to accompany Bob and me? We'll play bridge."

"Thanks, Agnes, but I plan to stay busy with my questioning, and I may leave early, so I'll need my car."

"Oh, take some time off for fun. Eat, drink and be merry. And don't let your feelings get hurt if people are rude. Everyone's been so touchy about this lawsuit lately!"

CALLIE FELT THE disapproval of the community as she walked from the hot, sunny parking lot toward the shady picnic area that overlooked the beach. Though she recognized many of the adults clustered around food-laden picnic tables and sizzling grills, no one smiled, waved or greeted her. Some stared. Some glanced away. Some leaned to mutter into another's ear.

The community had clearly closed its ranks against her. She'd expected as much. Both the sheriff and Agnes had warned her. She hadn't realized, though, how heavily the rejection would weigh on her heart.

What was the old saying…something about never being able to go home again? Funny. The beaches, the dunes, the water, the marina with its boats, the pavilion with its bandstand, all looked so much the same as when she'd belonged here.

She wanted to drive away, before the heaviness grew any more oppressive. But she couldn't leave without asking the women if they'd put shrimp in their dishes last July, or if anyone remembered anything that might prove remotely helpful in figuring out the true cause of Agnes's hallucinations.

Callie paused at the edge of the social hubbub, keeping her chin resolutely level and her expression pleasant.

Despite her dread of facing Jack in public, she wondered if he had arrived yet. She didn't see him or his family anywhere. She also didn't see any of the friends she'd considered her "gang"—Jimbo, Robbie or Frankie.

She did, however, notice Agnes in her yellow kimono seated at a table near the pavilion. A white-haired, dignified gentleman and three elderly ladies sat with her, playing cards. Callie started toward them, hoping to station herself near friendly territory before infiltrating the hostile crowd.

Conscious of the glances that followed her, she wondered if she'd made a mistake in her choice of apparel. She'd considered wearing her cutoffs, the only shorts she'd packed, but decided against it. Too clearly she remembered Jack's stirring recollections of her cutoffs, and the way he'd run his fingers across her bare thighs. She couldn't bring herself to wear them.

She'd chosen instead a simple white sundress. Casual, but not too casual. She wasn't here for fun and games, and wouldn't dress as if she were. No one else had worn a dress, though. Only shorts, jeans and bathing suits. She felt out of place, and the feeling only added to her sense of isolation.

"Callie Marshall?" At the cold voice, she turned to face a stern woman with a thin, plain countenance, dull brown hair tugged into a tight bun and vertical frown lines around her mouth and between her eyes. "I'm Flora Mulhollen, the school nurse."

"Yes, of course, Miss Mulhollen," Callie greeted warmly. They'd always called her *Miss Mole Hole*. "How are you?"

She ignored the courteous question. "I heard you're investigating the charge against Doctor Forrester. He saved Agnes's life, and it's a shame he's being slandered."

"I understand your concern. You may be able to help

clear his name. Did you attend the Fourth of July picnic?"

The woman pursed her lips, deepening their grooves. "I heard how you tricked Gloria into giving you photos to use against him. Your tricks won't work on me." Stiffly she marched off into the crowd.

Callie resisted the urge to glance around in embarrassment at the people who had been listening. Instead, she forced an amiable smile and struck up a determined conversation with the nearest group. No one there answered her inquiries with more than monosyllables, and when she asked if they'd put shrimp into their dishes last July, they all said they couldn't remember.

Perhaps she'd socialize for a while—break the ice—before she attempted any more questioning.

As she wove her way between picnic tables and clusters of chatting neighbors, an adolescent boy in swim trunks leaped up onto a vacant picnic table. "Look, look!" he shouted, pointing toward the marina. "Doc's bringing in his boat!"

A cheer went up. Children of all ages surged into a lively mob and ran toward the marina as a sleek white yacht motored across the green water toward an open boat slip. Mothers pulled back the smallest children and yelled for the older ones to keep a safe distance from the dock. Fathers sauntered along behind the kids, their own gazes fixed on the approaching pleasure craft.

Callie leaned against an unoccupied picnic table and watched.

The boat backed neatly into the slip. The first person she noticed on board was a petite, deeply tanned blonde, her platinum hair a bouncy shoulder-length, her vivacious smile brilliantly white as she waved from the back deck to the flock of children.

An invisible band tightened painfully around Callie's ribs. Had Jack brought a date to the picnic? Another woman, so soon after their lovemaking last night?

Two men leaped out from the enclosed wheelhouse and tied off the lines. Callie recognized the heftiest man, with his shock of spaghetti-red hair, as Jimbo. The other, who sported a dark ponytail and mustache, looked only vaguely familiar. As he smiled somewhat shyly at the crowd, she identified him as Robbie.

And when the petite blonde rammed a playful fist into Jimbo's massive arm, Callie knew she could be no other than Frankie, the only other female member of their childhood gang.

A tall, majestic, older couple emerged from the wheelhouse. Dr. and Mrs. Forrester. Jack's parents.

Callie's heart gave a painful lurch. She'd spent the happiest part of her childhood with these people. They'd known her better, in many ways, than her own sister or father had.

How would they receive her?

None of her old gang had phoned her since she'd returned, although they must have known she'd been back on the Point. She'd placed a call to Frankie yesterday and left a message on her recorder. Frankie hadn't returned the call.

Callie blamed herself. She hadn't kept in touch with her friends during her twelve-year absence. Why should they welcome her now? Especially when she'd come to investigate Jack, who had always been the unifying force behind their small, ragtag group.

At a sudden tugging on her dress, Callie glanced

down to find a pint-size boy with wide blue eyes and thick glasses gazing up at her. His arm, she noticed, was in a cast. "That's Doc's boat," he informed her with the most adorable lisp she'd ever heard. "My mom won't let me go by the dock because I fell in the water last time."

"Oh my."

"If I keep my cast dry, Doc's going to let me drive his boat next weekend."

"Really?"

He nodded earnestly and held up his cast. "He put this on my arm hisself. And I didn't cry."

Callie resisted the urge to ruffle his sandy-brown hair. "You're very brave."

"Doc says I'm the bravest he ever saw." He climbed up to sit on the table beside where she stood, then glanced toward the commotion at the marina. "There he is! There's Doc! See him?"

Callie's pulse sped up at the sight of a tall, tanned, golden-haired man moving among the people on the back deck of the boat. His deep laughter reached her through a cacophony of merry voices.

She turned away, suddenly desperate for a diversion, any diversion, to keep her occupied until her heart quit its ridiculous pounding.

"Mom, can I help Mrs. Forrester carry her picnic basket?" her newfound little friend called out.

"No, Kyle," replied a woman from another table. "It looks like she's got more help than she needs."

"Hey, there's Zeus!" Kyle exclaimed. "Doc brought his dog." A few playful barks confirmed the statement. "He has an alligator named Alfred, too, you know."

Keeping her back deliberately turned to the happy

babble of voices and joyful barking, Callie exclaimed in surprise, "He brought the alligator?"

Kyle stood up on the picnic-table bench and surveyed the scene. "Nope. Don't see him."

Callie murmured her relief, then gazed silently in the opposite direction from the commotion.

Although it would be awkward, she would have to greet her old friends, her seventh-grade teacher and the doctor who had treated her throughout her childhood. Mrs. Forrester had been more than her teacher, of course, and Dr. Forrester more than her doctor. Callie had been a regular visitor at their house. Whether they responded to her with warmth or coldness now, she would have to cordially greet them.

Soon, she told herself. After they'd settled down at a picnic table. Maybe after they'd eaten lunch...

The women setting up a buffet table of potluck dishes were surreptitiously watching her, she realized. From their curious, expectant gazes, she knew they were waiting to witness whatever interaction might take place between the Forresters and her. Any at all, including a lack of interaction, would be gossip worthy.

Perhaps she should take refuge with Agnes, her only ally.

That, however, would be cowardly.

Drawing a fortifying breath, she sat down at the picnic table with Kyle. She'd bide her time until she felt the moment was right to wander over to the Forresters and her childhood friends to say a courteous hello.

"So, uh, how did you break your arm, Kyle?" she asked.

He regaled her with the story of his fall from a tree. As she listened, Callie sneaked an occasional glance at

Mrs. Forrester and Frankie, who led a procession of boys carrying picnic baskets and coolers to the table directly across an open expanse of grass from where Callie sat.

Had they noticed her? Had they deliberately chosen the table farthest away?

She turned her attention to Kyle's animated description of his fall, complete with the sound of his bone breaking. Callie winced and murmured the appropriate sounds of awe.

The next time she glanced up, Mrs. Forrester and Frankie had spread tablecloths over two tables, while Jimbo, Robbie and old Dr. Forrester stood talking among a jovial group of men.

Jack himself leisurely ambled from the marina with a gaggle of children leaping, skipping and laughing around him. One small boy rode on his broad shoulders, two little girls held his hands, and the lanky adolescent boy who had announced his arrival walked backward in front of him, gesturing in animated conversation.

Jack's German shepherd pranced beside them with a red bandanna around his neck and his thick, black, coppery fur glistening in the September afternoon sunshine.

"Wanna see all the names people wrote on my cast?" Kyle held up his encased forearm proudly. Glad for the distraction, Callie listened as the boy deciphered each scribble.

"Excuse me," piped up a soft voice from beside them. A young girl with long dark braids stood shyly gazing at her. "Are you Miss Callie Marshall?"

A pang of apprehension went through her. "Yes."

"Mrs. Forrester wants to see you." The girl's voice

carried enough to seize the attention of every adult around them.

Aware that an audience now watched with blatant interest, Callie nervously glanced across the grassy clearing at the woman who had summoned her. Looking slim and elegant in a neat beige blouse and summer slacks, Mrs. Forrester stood with her arms folded, her head high and her stern gaze locked on Callie.

"Uh-oh," whispered Kyle, his eyes wide behind his glasses. "That's the principal of my school. I think you're in trouble."

Callie swallowed against a suddenly dry throat. She thought so, too. No student of Mrs. Forrester's would ever take her summons lightly. And no one who knew her as a mother would expect her to tolerate an attack against her son. She'd always been one of his staunchest supporters.

Callie would now stand before her as one of his detractors.

She tried to force a smile but wasn't sure she succeeded. Rising on rubbery legs, she walked across the grass, aware that the people surrounding Mrs. Forrester had fallen silent.

Everyone seemed to be watching.

As Callie grew closer, she saw that her honey-blond hair, caught up in its usual soft twist, now glinted lightly with gray, and the lines around her brown eyes were more pronounced, but she wore the same air of regal elegance and authority that had awed generations of students.

"I understand, Ms. Marshall," she said in her smooth Southern voice that somehow straightened one's posture, "that you've come to the Point on business."

"Yes, ma'am."

A very subtle lifting of one honey-blond brow and a disapproving stare ambushed Callie with regret. Though she'd leveled a few punishments against her in the classroom and always sided with the Colonel whenever Callie had complained about his stifling rules, Mrs. Forrester had believed in her. She'd seen merit in all of her work and encouraged her to aim high. And when her mother had died, Mrs. Forrester had come to Callie's house and held her. Simply held her.

"The work that brought me to the Point," Callie haltingly explained, "is just business. Nothing personal."

"Obviously, since you haven't seen fit to grace us with your presence."

Callie hesitated, confused by the remark. "Ma'am?"

Mrs. Forrester inclined her head in her most teacherlike manner. "From what I understand, young lady, you've been here for two days. Have you called any of us? Hmm?"

A hand raised and wagged energetically in the air beside Callie. "Oh, oh, I know, Ms. Forrester," cried Frankie, her arm extended above her sleek blond head like a rambunctious student's. "She called *me*. But I didn't check my messages until this morning." She turned to Callie with a typical Frankie shrug and grin. "Sorry, Cal."

"She didn't call *me*," Jimbo complained loudly in his hefty, gruff, he-man voice.

"Me neither, man." Robbie regarded her with a comically doleful frown beneath the bushy mustache he'd sprouted since she'd last seen him twelve years ago. "I'm totally bummed."

Callie stared at the familiar faces, too stunned by their teasing, welcoming warmth to speak.

Mrs. Forrester put an arm around Callie's waist, drew her closer and angled her toward the picnic table. "I guess the question is, should old acquaintance be forgot?"

"Hey, that's your cue, Freddie!" Jimbo yelled.

A saxophone struck up the tune "Auld Lang Syne." A chorus of zestful voices joined in, only slightly off-key. Arms wove around shoulders and the group swayed around the table.

Through a disbelieving daze, Callie noticed the chocolate sheet cake in front of her sprinkled with candy confetti. Yellow frosting spelled out, "Welcome Home, Callie."

Her throat clenched. Her eyes misted. She wouldn't cry! Especially not in front of Jimbo and Robbie. The last, lingering trace of tomboy in her wouldn't allow it. The big-city career woman she'd become wouldn't allow it. She looked away from the cake, the singers and the smiles, fighting for control.

Her gaze veered to Jack.

He was leaning against a tall, smooth-barked palm tree, watching her with the pleasant detachment of an amiable stranger. How did he feel about this extravagant welcome his mother and friends had extended her? His bland expression gave no hint.

But he wasn't standing among them, his arms looped across friends' shoulders, his voice raised in song. He stood apart from the action—very unlike the Jack Forrester she'd always known—a fact that had to be noted by the other residents of Moccasin Point who looked on in interest.

Not that anyone would blame him. She was, after all,

the investigator who had been seeking damaging facts and photos to destroy his good name.

No one knew he'd been her lover last night; the one who had turned her heart inside out with the most sumptuous passion she'd ever known.

She supposed she should be grateful for his aloof yet pleasant air, regardless of what feelings, if any, he harbored. She'd begged for his discretion, and he was giving it to her.

Yet she couldn't help wishing for a sign—the smallest of smiles, the most discreet of nods—to tell her he didn't mind this public display of welcome, the warm and wonderful taste of friendship she'd thought lost forever, the camaraderie that lifted her heart as nothing else could have.

The song ended. Mrs. Forrester hugged her. "You do whatever business you have to, but don't be a stranger, hear?"

"Mrs. Forrester," Callie whispered, anxiously searching her eyes, "you do know the nature of my business, don't you?"

"Of course. But I have faith in him, and in you, too. You'll do whatever's right. Now go have fun."

Frankie spun her around with an exuberant "I can't believe you're wearing a *dress*. I didn't recognize you. You look gorgeous! Robbie, come take a picture of Callie in this dress."

A camera flashed, and when her vision cleared, Robbie grinned and winked. Jimbo shoved him aside, looked Callie up and down, then let out a long, low whistle. "Never thought I'd see the day, Marshall." A teasing, obnoxious smile spread across his wide, slightly freckled face. "You look so good, I might have to give you a big ol' wet kiss."

She gripped two fistfuls of his sleeveless black T-shirt. "Try it, Henderson, and you'll be picking teeth out of your tonsils." She punctuated that promise with a shove against his meaty chest.

Jimbo shouted a laugh. "Good golly, it *is* you, Marshall."

"Come on, Cal. I want you to meet my husband." Frankie hooked her arm through Callie's and led her across the grass. "By the way, I go by 'Francine' now."

"Oh, right, *Frankie*," Jimbo scoffed.

Frankie flipped him her middle finger in a rude but discreet gesture behind her back as she ushered Callie toward another lively cluster of picnickers.

Jack watched from his post by the palm tree, wondering if Callie would risk another glance at him.

She didn't. She'd given him just that one dazed stare in the middle of the song. He'd been glad to see that the hurt, little-girl-lost expression had left her eyes, though he doubted anyone else had seen it through the veil of cool dignity she wore so well.

Her need to hide behind a veil of any kind angered him. In a misguided attempt to show him support, the community had shut her out.

At least his parents and close friends had more sense than to think he'd want Callie snubbed, regardless of her mission. They'd jumped at his suggestion of a cake, which his mother had baked and decorated yesterday. Frankie had thought of the song, and Jimbo had arranged for Freddie of The Flounders to play it.

Jack wasn't sure why he himself had hung back from the welcome-home celebration. Maybe because he knew she wasn't home to stay. Maybe because that fact was eating a hole through him.

Tearing his gaze away from her alluring profile as

she shook hands with Frankie's husband, Jack opened a cooler and dug a can of beer from the ice, more for an outward show of party spirit than from any real desire for the beer. He wouldn't doubt she'd take a picture of him drinking it to add to her collection.

He flipped the tab up with his thumb and resisted the urge to follow her again with his eyes. Not an easy thing to resist, when he craved the sight of her. And the feel. And the taste.

He took a deep, unsatisfying swig of beer.

Last night hadn't been what he'd expected.

Oh, he hadn't been too surprised by the gut-torching passion. He'd felt his first stunning blast of it when he'd kissed her earlier. And he hadn't been too overwhelmed by the beauty of her naked body, though it had, admittedly, rocked him with some force. He'd always known he'd find her beautiful.

But he hadn't expected the surge after surge of hot emotion that crested through him the entire time he'd made love to her. And he hadn't expected that emotion to stay with him, like a low-grade fever, long after he'd torn himself away from her bed.

He hadn't yet recovered.

Worse, though, was this morning-after anxiety he'd never before experienced. What if last night had been all he could ever have of her? He couldn't forget the last coherent words she'd spoken: *Never, ever, ever…*

The can of beer buckled in at one side beneath his clenching fingers, and foam sloshed over his hand.

The idea of never kissing her, or holding her, or loving her again, was too intolerable to entertain.

You scared her off, an inner voice charged.

He suspected that was true. He had known why she'd stopped him during their lovemaking—at least, until he'd overcome her hesitation with stark, physical need. She'd panicked because of the emotional intensity he hadn't been able to hide. She'd wanted to play. He'd wanted to seize and possess and consume.

God help him, he still did.

He had to keep his distance, he realized, until he got himself under control. Until he knew he could interact with her in a light, casual, rational way that wouldn't send her running back to Tallahassee.

"Hey, Doc, we found the seine net," said one of the teenage boys he'd sent to rummage through his fishing gear on the boat. A lively mob of younger kids, who had been romping on the beach with Zeus, caught sight of the seine net and raced over with eager smiles.

Thank God for diversions.

He tossed the half-full can of beer into a trash bin and led his bevy of young fishermen to the beach.

THE LUMP THAT HAD LODGED in Callie's throat showed no signs of diminishing. Frankie and Mrs. Forrester introduced her to their friends, some of whom she'd known long ago. Dr. Forrester—Jack's ginger-haired, robust father—acknowledged her with a wink and nod, then settled his large frame into a lounge chair with his pipe and the *Wall Street Journal.*

She felt dazed by the warmth they'd all shown her. Honored. Grateful.

Confused.

She'd assumed that Jack's family and closest friends would turn a cold shoulder to her. She'd been prepared to deal with that. Not until they'd sprung their surprise celebration had she realized how much their acceptance meant to her.

She felt, for the first time since her mother had died, that she'd come home.

A dangerous feeling, especially when her head and heart still reeled from her night with Jack. She couldn't allow herself to get too attached to her rediscovered friends, or to the balmy, tranquil place of her childhood, or to the orthopedic surgeon who now engaged an adoring group of children in a lively attempt to trap mullet.

She'd made her home in Tallahassee and, with her busy schedule, probably wouldn't return here very often. More importantly, she had a job to finish that could hurt these very people.

She tried to keep all that in mind as she and Frankie settled into lounge chairs with raspberry wine coolers and chatted about their lives over the past twelve years.

A trio of ladies interrupted them and confronted Callie with determined expressions. "I heard you've been asking about shrimp at our picnic last July," said Betty Gallagher, the sheriff's wife. "Thought you should know that I put some in my cheese biscuits."

"Your cheese biscuits?" Callie repeated in surprise. Agnes *had* mentioned sampling some of those, which meant her allergic reaction had been real, and Jack's injection *had* saved her life.

"And I threw a few into my Hawaiian-style pineapple fruit salad," chimed in Louise Cavanaugh.

"I shredded some into my coleslaw," added another woman.

Callie gazed at them in mild suspicion. Either they were making false claims to validate Jack's emergency treatment of Agnes, or poor Agnes had had plenty of reason to turn purple. "Well, that clears up the shrimp question," she announced, visibly pleasing them all.

When the women trooped away, Frankie broached the subject she'd been avoiding. "I have to admit, Cal, I didn't know what to think when I first heard about your investigation. I could understand Meg accepting the case, since she never hung around with us much as kids, but you and Jack were always so tight."

Callie stared down into the pinkish depths of her wine cooler. "I have a business to run. Payroll to meet. Important clients to please. Meg is one of those clients."

"Don't you care if you ruin Jack's name?"

She lifted her gaze to meet Frankie's. She wanted to tell her that she wasn't the one suing Jack, and that she intended to search for only the truth, and that it would be up to Meg to decide if and how to pursue the case.

No words emerged from her mouth.

She couldn't talk about Jack right now. Whenever her gaze strayed toward the beach and she saw his golden hair gleaming in the sun, his bronzed arms rippling with muscle as he worked the net through the waves and his brilliant smile encouraging his young helpers, her heart spun in dizzying circles.

His hair had gleamed by the light of her bedside lamp last night, his muscles had rippled as he'd made love to her, and his smile had followed her into her dreams.

He hadn't said the first word to her yet today. Maybe he wouldn't. She should be glad.

Before she managed to pull her gaze away from Jack's distant figure, Frankie tactfully changed the subject.

WHILE THE BOYS CLEANED the mullet they'd caught and their mothers grilled the fillets, Jack showered and changed on his yacht, then returned to the throng of picnickers. A plate of grilled fish, barbecued ribs, casseroles and salads was thrust into his hands.

He settled down at a table beside his father.

A stream of friends paused at their table to joke, chat or just pat Jack on the back. Others exchanged witticisms with him from neighboring tables. One pretty young redhead tossed flirtatious smiles his way—a friend of a friend, he supposed—while a local beauty in tight black shorts sat down beside him, her thigh snug against his, her smile a blatant invitation.

To all appearances, he was having a high old time.

Except he couldn't stop his gaze from following the slender brunette in the white sundress who refused to pay him the slightest attention. She carried a plate from the buffet, and Jack noticed men's secretive glances at her while she strolled by. His muscles tensed with a possessiveness that startled him.

He really couldn't blame them for watching. She was so damn beautiful, he ached just looking at her.

The white, strapless sundress hugged her breasts and narrow waist, then flowed in gauzy folds that silhouetted her mile-long legs. Her dark, thick hair shimmered in tousled waves, inviting a man's fingers to sift through them. And her hips moved with the same sensuous grace that had slain him as a teenager.

He knew those hips intimately now. He'd held them last night while he'd lunged deeply into her. Her body had turned to hot, fluid silk around him.

He glanced away. Clenched his jaw. Struggled for control. No wonder he'd scared her. The mere memory of making love to her ignited him with a fearsome intensity that scared even him.

He couldn't keep his eyes away from her.

She'd chosen a seat at a distant table with Frankie, his mother and a few other women. Only one male had joined the group—little Kyle Talmidge, his thick glasses crooked on his face and his arm cast propped on the table. He'd somehow wriggled himself into the small space beside Callie. She gifted him with a tender smile.

Never before had Jack felt envious of a six-year-old.

If he didn't find a way to win a smile for himself, or to touch her or maybe even hold her, he wasn't sure he could make it through the rest of the picnic.

A kiss would help ease the peculiar tension gripping him. A long, private kiss. His temperature rose at the prospect.

"You okay, son?"

Jack shifted his attention to his father, who'd been eating in companionable silence beside him. "I'm fine. Why?"

His father swung a slow, pointed gaze toward Callie. "Oh, I don't know." He pushed his plate away, drew a redolent cherry-wood pipe from his shirt pocket and struck a match.

A man of few words but remarkable insight.

Jack realized then that the flirtatious beauty who'd been sitting too close on his other side had left the table. The food piled on his plate remained virtually untouched. And the icy can of beer someone had placed in his hand now sagged with a dent in its side. Suds streamed down onto his fingers.

He sorely needed that kiss from Callie.

"Freddie," he called to his longhaired musician friend at the next table. "I'd say it's time for some dance music."

THE FIRST HINT OF EVENING had cooled the air and splashed the sky with pink and violet. Parents with children said their goodbyes. Teenagers congregated on the beach to build a bonfire.

Freddie and the Flounders, meanwhile, nearly raised the roof off the pavilion with a rollicking blend of country-western and rock. Couples danced the two-step, the swing and their own freestyle gyrations across the pavilion floor while spectators hooted, whistled and clapped. Frankie, Jimbo and Robbie grabbed their partners and joined in the festivities.

Callie watched from the crowded sidelines, hoping she wouldn't be asked to dance. She'd never been very good at it.

Besides, she was simply waiting for the chance to say goodbye to her friends. The time had come for her to go.

She'd noticed during dinner that two pretty women had been hovering around Jack. No one could mistake the invitation in either woman's smile. Would he take one of them up on the invitation? Why shouldn't he?

Pain had lanced through Callie at that thought, and she'd resolutely kept her gaze away from him. She'd also overheard disturbing snatches of conversation in the crowd behind her.

"Mrs. Forrester was just being gracious. Have you noticed that Doc himself hasn't said a word to her?" "I don't blame him for keeping his distance." "I don't believe he gave her his car to drive yesterday. That rumor can't be true."

Callie realized that if she were thinking straight, she wouldn't mind those speculations. Hadn't she prayed that no one would find out about her relationship with Jack? Hadn't she begged him to keep their night together a secret?

Why, then, did her heart ache at his continued aloofness? As much as she hated to admit it, she'd been longing all day for one of his smiles, or a warm glance. Or a touch.

She closed her eyes with a strong, sudden desire to feel his touch. To be held in his arms. To stare into his heated, golden-brown eyes and make hard, sweaty love to him.

Her breath caught in her throat and she forced the image from her mind. She couldn't allow herself to crave him this way. But even as she thought it, she opened her eyes and involuntarily searched the crowd for him.

She saw him nowhere.

Frankie danced by with her husband. Robbie shuffled by with his date. Sheriff Gallagher and his daughter two-stepped past her, and unfamiliar couples whirled across the floor.

The song ended, and a new one began. Although the tempo was fairly lively, the poetic lyrics spoke of a powerful, forever kind of love. She didn't want to listen.

She turned to leave, but before she could, a broad chest in a crisp white shirt blocked her way. She drew back, breathing in the sudden whiff of a familiar masculine scent that made her heart stand still. Blood drummed in her ears. Her temperature rose.

A savagely handsome, scarred face filled her vision, and golden-brown eyes captured hers.

With a nod at the dance floor beside them, Jack opened his arms. "Callie," he said, the intensity of his gaze contradicting his courteous smile, "may I?"

9

"NO, NO, I...I DON'T DANCE. I'm not very good at it. I—"

"What's the matter, Cal?" His arm lightly corralled her, encircling her waist, drawing her closer. "Scared?"

"Of course not, but—"

"I dare you." Jack's gaze blazed across her face like a beam of summer heat. "Double dare," he whispered.

He wasn't playing fair. Her personal sense of pride wouldn't let the challenge go unanswered, as he well knew. Jimbo's face loomed up beside them on the dance floor, watching them with unabashed interest as he and his date danced by. The crowd around them seemed to be watching, too.

Hesitantly Callie laid her hand on his shoulder and the other into his extended palm. She braced herself, aware of the attention they'd drawn, and the breathless dizziness his nearness had caused, and the heat streaming through her from his touch.

He allowed none of her stiffness or distance. He pulled her firmly against him and guided her onto the floor, where he held her gaze with a smiling warmth that rushed to her head like fine champagne.

For the first time in her life, she didn't look down at her feet or concentrate on her partner's moves. She couldn't take her eyes from his, and somehow forgot she was dancing at all. He coaxed her into a rhythm with smooth yet playful grace. Her body soon moved in easy, natural harmony with his.

He lifted her hand higher and led her into bolder moves, forcing her to smile at unexpected dips and turns. Before long, they were whirling through a maze of other couples, the skirt of her sundress billowing behind her and wrapping around his jean-clad legs. When they'd reached an empty corner, he twirled her out, then under his arm. He even leaned her dramatically backward, and she laughed out loud.

He pulled her up, caught her to him and held her still against his chest. Her eyes returned to his, and the heat, the intensity, nearly overpowered his smile. "Don't be afraid of doing anything with me, Callie."

Her heart pounded too high in her throat for her to answer, even to herself, as she succumbed to his golden-hot stare.

The music changed to a slow, evocative love song. Neither gave a thought to leaving the floor. His arm banded tighter around her, and his hand roamed the length of her back, molding her against him. She closed her eyes and pressed her cheek to his shoulder, savoring the familiar hardness and warmth beneath his cotton shirt.

They did little more than sway. And drink in the feel, the scent, the need. Strain closer together in sensuous gyrations. Hunger for more.

He angled his face near the side of her jaw and inhaled deeply, as if to breathe in her fragrance and hold it inside of him to better savor it. "God, I've missed you."

She knew what he meant, although they'd been within sight distance of each other all day. She'd missed him, too. She'd craved him…his touch, his warmth, his attention. A tingle of alarm went through her. She shouldn't be needing him this badly.

His mouth brushed against her ear, setting off a shower of hot sparks within her. "Meet me on my boat, Callie," he rasped. "We'll go offshore and anchor down for the night."

Her breath suspended somewhere between her heart and her head. She could spend another night with him! In his arms, in his bed.

"No one has to know, Cal," he breathed.

Temptation scalded her insides.

He drew back and foraged her gaze with blatant hunger. "Slip away as soon as you can. I'll be waiting there, no matter how long—"

"Excuse me." A cultured, masculine voice interrupted from very close beside them.

Jack turned his head with a questioning frown.

Grant Tierney lifted a dark, winged brow above glittering blue eyes. A smile curled his mouth. "May I cut in?"

Jack stiffened into utter stillness. Callie felt the muscles of his body turn to steel, saw his scarred face freeze into a mask of deadly warning. "No, you may not."

"I'd say that's up to the lady, wouldn't you?"

"You're not going to touch her."

Callie stared at the two men as if she'd been abruptly woken from a dream. She'd been so deeply immersed in her heated communion with Jack that she'd forgotten the rest of the world existed. She wanted nothing more than to wave Grant aside like a pesky mosquito and slip back into the sweet, sensuous dream.

But the cold, real world awaited her. Grant Tierney was an important part of that cold reality.

Every eye seemed focused on them. The other couples on the floor had stopped dancing. Jimbo and Robbie had pressed slightly forward, their expressions tense and watchful.

Jack's arms had turned granite hard around Callie, and his seething stare remained aimed at Grant.

Grant shifted a meaningful gaze to Callie. "Does he speak for you?"

The full impact of the situation hit her. She was caught between two violently opposing forces, and though they clashed over a simple dance, the confrontation represented much more to both of them. Her choice would grant one a public moral victory.

Which made her a kind of trophy. Or a pawn in their game.

The music stopped. The bandleader announced in jarringly cheerful tones, "I think we'll take a little break now, folks. We'll be back in about ten minutes with lots more music." As Freddie and his Flounders filed from the bandstand, the silence was broken only by whispers and murmurs from the watching crowd.

Clenching her jaw, Callie looked beyond Jack, beyond Grant, and murmured to no one in particular, "Looks like I'll have to take a rain check." She broke away from the suffocating glare of attention and plunged through a jungle of shoulders and faces.

"CALLIE! CALLIE, WAIT." Frankie banged on the passenger window of the Mercedes just as Callie began to back out of the parking space. "I need to talk to you."

Callie stopped the car, although she wasn't in the mood to talk. Her head spun and her heart ached with painful doubts. The fierce undertones of Jack's confrontation with Grant had made her feel as if she'd become a trophy in the game between them, or maybe just another bone for them to fight over.

Frankie opened the door, slid into the passenger seat and gazed at her in patent concern. "Callie, honey, you can't just run out on us like this. You're obviously upset, but I'm not sure—" She stopped and glanced around the luxurious, aromatic leather interior. "Wow, nice car."

"It's not mine." Callie gripped the wheel and stared blindly through the windshield into the evening shadows. "It's Meg's. I drive a nice, mid-sized Chevy that has never given me problems. And I live in a nice two-bedroom condo—good security, but nothing flashy. And I've been dating a nice accountant whom I've known for a month. Nothing too hot and heavy, mind you..." Her voice broke, and she squeezed her trembling lips together.

She'd had a taste of "hot and heavy," and knew she wouldn't find it with anyone other than Jack. Nor did she want to. Passion that made her too dizzy to think belonged in the same class with flashy, high-powered cars. Not her style. More than she could afford. Potentially dangerous.

"Why are you running away again, Cal?"

"Running away?" She swung a protesting glance to Frankie. "You've got it backward. I'm going home where I belong. To *my* life. The one I built." In a whisper to herself, she added, "The one I understand."

A troubled look shadowed Frankie's blue eyes. "Jack sent me with a message. He said to meet him."

Callie stared at her, too choked up to respond. He was waiting for her on his boat. To take her offshore, anchor down and make love to her. *I'll be waiting there*, he'd whispered, *no matter how long...*

She closed her eyes and leaned her forehead against the steering wheel. Even with painful suspicions digging into her heart, she still wanted to go to him.

With a flash of clarity, she realized the god-awful truth. She was falling in love with him!

The realization twisted her insides into knots. She'd worked too hard to grow from the unskilled, insecure, financially broke, emotionally shattered girl who'd left the Point. She'd survived both the Colonel's and Jack's emotional abandonment, and strengthened herself on all fronts to prevent ever falling prey to that pain again.

But now that pain had come knocking on her door. She couldn't let it in!

"Tell Jack I won't be able to make it. And tell him, also, please—" a mist sprang to her eyes and she blinked it away "—that if he cares about me at all, he won't contact me again."

A bleak silence settled between them.

"I'm not sure what's going on, Cal, but from what I saw on the dance floor, you definitely feel something for him. And Jack, well, I've never seen him in this state. He's usually the king of cool. Now he seems more like a powder keg."

"Don't you understand why?"

"Because he's crazy about you?"

Callie shook her head, too overwrought to explain that Jack's powerful emotions stemmed more from his rivalry with Grant than from anything he felt about her, whether Jack fully realized it or not.

He'd admitted hating the fact that she worked on Grant's behalf. The Jack Forrester she'd always known would take that as a challenge to win her over to his side for the world to see. She thought back to the first time he'd kissed her—right after his outrage over the prospect of her attending the picnic with Grant. Suddenly Jack had found her irresistible. He'd kissed her in front of Gloria, climbed onto her balcony with disregard for the neighbors, and now made a spectacle of her on the dance floor.

You were just as much to blame, her conscience whispered. She couldn't deny that. She also had to admit the possibility that his motives stemmed from a chivalrous desire to save her from the man who had nearly destroyed his sister. On the other hand, his pursuit of her could be chalked up to just another macho showdown with his rival.

Either way, Grant Tierney figured prominently in Jack's motivation.

"Callie, I believe Jack needs you."

"I don't want to hear anything more about him." She was confused enough as it was.

"If you care about him at all, you'd better listen." Frankie's sharp tone acted almost as a slap, drawing both Callie's resentment and attention. "We've all been worried about him. He takes his work too much to heart and bottles up the emotions. Like a couple of months ago, he operated on a little boy with a spinal injury. Jack did everything he could, but the injury was too serious. The boy probably won't walk again."

Despite her resolve to remain unaffected, sympathy squeezed Callie's heart. If she'd reacted this way from simply hearing about the boy's prognosis, she could imagine how Jack had felt.

"Jack thinks he's learned to accept the problems he can't fix," Frankie said, "but I don't believe he has. During his free time, he seems driven to gather people around him, which he does so easily. But then he never really connects with anyone. He cuts out in the middle of parties and takes off in his boat alone."

"He probably takes a woman with him." Callie couldn't help thinking of his suggestion to her, and the fact that he waited for her now.

"Nope. The women are always present and accounted for."

The stab of relief only disturbed Callie more. "What does any of that have to do with me?"

"He connects with you, Callie. Heck, even when we were kids, you two had a special understanding of each other, and we all knew it. Now that you've come back, he's showing signs of real life again. My gosh, the way he looked at you and held you on the dance floor—"

"The connection we've had since I've come back," Callie said, desperate to make her understand the true nature of their relationship, "is sex. Just sex."

Her friend stared at her in surprise. "Well, that's a start."

"That's also the end."

Frankie released a frustrated breath and dropped her hands into her lap. "Because of Tierney's lawsuit, right?" She twisted her mouth and shook her head. "As frivolous as it is, this suit will end up hurting Jack more than the other one did."

Callie stiffened. "The other one?"

"The Sharon Landers case." The words had barely left her mouth when she froze, winced and shot Callie a patently regretful glance, as if she wished she could recall the words. "Y-you can't use a previous lawsuit against Jack, can you?" stuttered Frankie. "I mean, it wasn't his fault. No one even *implied* the error was his fault."

Dismay washed through Callie in cold, strong currents. A previous lawsuit would certainly be pertinent to the investigation, and to withhold it from Meg would constitute a definite breach of her contract. "Don't feel bad about telling me, Frankie. I would have found out about it anyway. The computer checks I planned to run this week would have brought it to my attention." Hoping against hope, she asked through a tightened throat, "Was it a frivolous lawsuit? Something nonsensical?"

"Well, no." After a long pause, Frankie released an unhappy sigh. "But please believe that it wasn't Jack's fault. He was one of three surgeons working on a woman after an automobile accident. While he operated on her leg, a plastic surgeon fixed her face. The chief surgeon was overseeing the whole procedure. Somehow, the anesthesiologist accidentally disconnected her breathing tube." Frankie looked out the window for a moment, then murmured, "She never regained consciousness."

"She died?"

Frankie nodded. "Her husband sued the hospital, along with all the doctors who had worked on her. They settled the case out of court to keep it quiet. Jack was devastated by the woman's death. He felt he should have realized that something had gone wrong. But heck, he was only in his first year of residency."

Callie ached to think how much the death must have affected him. She ached even more to think of how he would feel if the case were brought up in court. And to know that *she* had submitted the information.

"Look, Cal. I know it's your job to investigate Jack, but sometimes personal matters have to take priority over career decisions." Callie opened her mouth to argue, and Frankie held up a staying hand. "Maybe this isn't one of those times." She reached across the seat and squeezed Callie's arm. "But then again, maybe it is. Think about it, okay?"

Callie nodded, unable to speak.

Frankie climbed from the car and shut the door. But after she'd taken a few steps, she turned around and leaned into Callie's open window. "And please, *please*, don't mention the Sharon Landers lawsuit to anyone. It happened when he was working in Miami and not many people around here know about it. I only know because his mother told me. Jack still gets this bleak look in his eyes when it's mentioned."

Callie felt the bleakness herself—in the pit of her stomach. Frankie smiled rather sadly and strode away.

As Callie shook herself out of painful reflection and reached for the button to close the window, a tall shadow separated from a nearby palm tree and ambled toward her. The light from the overhead security lamp fell across a pale, aristocratic face and gleaming black hair.

Grant Tierney.

He leaned his arm against the roof of her car and smiled down at her. "Just wanted to extend you my compliments. You're doing an excellent job."

JACK PACED ACROSS the back deck of his yacht and watched the marina's softly lit walkways for Callie. Would she meet him?

Anxiety balled up like a fist in his chest.

She'd been upset when she'd run from the dance floor. He couldn't blame her. She'd asked for his discretion, and he'd dragged her into the spotlight, center stage.

He gritted his teeth with painful force. He should have let Tierney dance with her. But even now, the thought of Tierney holding Callie in his arms repelled him beyond bearing.

He'd seen too many women succumb to some incomprehensible lure of Tierney's, and land squarely under his thumb. The impulse to snatch her away from the potential danger had overruled his common sense. But it hadn't been an entirely protective instinct that had pushed him to challenge Tierney. He'd also been seized by sheer, gut-wrenching possessiveness.

He wanted Callie for himself. She was his, made by God for him alone. He wouldn't have his enemy touching her.

Still reeling from the volcanic force of that sentiment, Jack shut his eyes and dropped down into a chair. When the hell had he reached the conclusion that Callie belonged to him? When he'd first kissed her and knew his life wouldn't be complete without making love to her? When he'd made love to her and realized he wanted much, much more than sex? When he woke up this morning, craving her company with a profound hunger, heartsick that she'd be leaving him?

He wasn't sure when, or even why, but he was damn sure of one thing: he'd fallen in love with her. She'd only been home for three days—three days!—yet he knew he'd never stop wanting her, or needing the uncanny bond between them that fulfilled a fierce need in his soul.

Could a feeling this strong be entirely one-sided?

He couldn't imagine it. He'd felt the awesome passion in her kisses, in her lovemaking. In her gazes. Maybe all she needed was time to comprehend the magnitude of what that passion meant.

Yet every instinct in him warned that he'd lose her if he made the wrong move. He'd already scared her during their lovemaking last night and sent her running from the dance floor this evening.

How could he have been such a damn fool as to cause a public scene? He'd avoided her all day, fortifying his self-control for the moment he would finally talk to her. And touch her. And dance with her. He'd been determined to strike the right note of warm nonchalance.

But then he took her in his arms and held her to his heart and lost all perspective.

Another flare of self-directed anger increased the painful pressure in his chest. He'd made a terrible mistake by showing Tierney his hand. An unholy awareness had sparkled in the bastard's eyes.

Jack had deprived him of a bride at his last wedding. Tierney would now take delight in depriving Jack of Callie. And he would have many opportunities to try. She worked for him; at least, until she finished this damn investigation.

Tierney had found the perfect weapon to use against him—the woman he loved. The very fact that he had the power to interfere with their relationship at such a vulnerable stage infuriated Jack.

He struggled with the impulse to find Callie, physically carry her aboard his boat, set course for the open seas and keep her with him until she realized she couldn't live without him.

He supposed that might not be the smartest of strategies.

The sound of footsteps on the dock brought him to his feet and sped up his heart. Had she come? Maybe he'd have his chance tonight. Maybe he'd make such incredible love to her that by morning, she'd never want to leave him.

A slight, feminine figure rounded the corner. Frankie.

She stopped on the dock beside his yacht and gazed at him in hesitant silence. "I'm sorry, Jack. Callie went back to the inn. She said to tell you she can't make it tonight, and that, uh, if you care about her at all—" she winced and finished with grave reluctance "—you won't contact her again."

The most extraordinary pain robbed him of the capacity to answer. *If he cared about her at all.* Did she doubt that? And was this to be his way to prove it...by never contacting her again?

"It sounds like she's planning to leave the Point soon," Frankie said. "Back to 'her life,' as she called it."

Her life. The one in which he played no part. She really did mean to leave him behind.

"Jack, I hate to sound unsympathetic, but that was some scene you caused on the dance floor. You really put her on the spot, expecting her to choose between publicly humiliating you or her business associate."

He felt a flush rise beneath his skin, but from emotions more painful than embarrassment. He hadn't meant to force Callie into a public declaration of where her loyalties lay. But obviously he'd done just that.

Obviously she hadn't chosen him.

"You should be thankful that it's Callie running this investigation for Tierney," Frankie went on. "She'll look for the truth, which can only be good for you. And I'm sure she believes you're innocent of the accusation."

Jack clenched his jaw and stared out into the star-brilliant night. No matter how Callie might affect the outcome of the lawsuit, he didn't want her involved with it. And he didn't necessarily need for her to believe he was innocent.

He wanted her on his side, whether she thought he was right or wrong. Whether a court determined he'd made a medical mistake or not. Whether he ended up paying a fortune in damages or walking away with a clear name.

He wanted her crazy in love with him.

He wanted it so much he felt ready to explode.

Although he'd never before dealt with this particular kind of pain or unrelenting emotional pressure, he knew how to regain control of himself. He simply needed time alone and plenty of personal space. The wind in his hair. The challenge of the sea.

He managed a fair simulation of a smile and sent Frankie back to the party with his promise to cause no more scenes. He then guided his boat through the channel and into the open gulf.

But this time, he found no distracting thrill in fighting the turbulent waves. The open air granted him no "personal space." The wind in his hair only made him colder. And the solitude only sharpened his loneliness and sense of utter loss.

"WITHDRAWING FROM the investigation! Are you crazy?"

Callie winced at Meg's shout and held the phone slightly away from her ear. She'd thought about this call all night, and had imagined those exact words. She felt as if she'd heard them a dozen times. "I'm sorry, Meg, but I won't change my mind about this. I shouldn't have accepted the case in the first place."

"Are you forgetting how much business Grant and

Agnes Tierney can pump through this law firm? Their corporate work alone could mean a partnership for me. And if I'm made a partner, I will guarantee that most of our investigative needs will be channeled through your firm. It's worth finishing up with this investigation, isn't it?"

"I've, uh, lost my objectivity."

"Your what?"

Callie struggled to find her voice. Somehow she'd lost that, too. The bright morning light had brought no end to her emotional turmoil. She wanted to see him again, hold him again, with a greater need than ever.

And she fervently hoped that Grant Tierney hadn't overheard Frankie telling her about the Sharon Landers case. She couldn't bear to think about that information being used against Jack.

"Callie, this isn't about Jack Forrester, is it?"

"Yes," she whispered.

"You've seen him? Talked to him?"

"Uh-huh."

"He reminded you of the good ol' days and made you feel guilty for taking the case against him, right?"

"Not exactly. Well, maybe." Callie closed her eyes and tried to voice her thoughts in a coherent manner. "I just don't believe he was guilty of malpractice, and I want no part in destroying his good name."

"I can't believe this! You've let him dazzle you with that killer smile of his, and now—"

"I thought you said you barely remembered him."

"That's about all I do remember. He really knew how to flash a girl a smile. A real ladies' man. But I thought you were impervious to that kind of thing."

"I won't argue about this, Meg. I'm off the case."

"You realize how the senior partners of the firm are

going to take this, don't you? When I tell them that we have to hire another investigator, they'll think you're unreliable. They won't trust you with anything important. At worst, they could sue you for breach of contract. The word will spread, Callie, and you'll be lucky to get a case from any law firm in town."

"Then maybe I'll finish law school and give you attorneys a run for your money."

"I thought you gave up on a law degree."

"No, I just got too busy trying to earn a living."

"A living is a wonderful thing," Meg reminded her. "Can you at least turn over whatever you've found on the case?"

"No."

"No?" she repeated in surprise. An awkward silence stretched between them. When she spoke again, her voice sounded hesitant and concerned. "Callie, you're not seriously falling in love with him or anything, are you?"

She couldn't bring herself to answer.

"Callie?" When she received no reply, Meg exhaled a long, hard breath. "I hope you're not setting yourself up for heartbreak. I mean, I'd be thrilled if you found a good man to share your life with, but I don't remember Jack Forrester as the stable, dependable type. And in this situation, it's clearly to his advantage to manipulate your emotions."

"Don't worry about me, Meg," Callie said, trying for a reassuring tone. "I'm almost over him already. I'm coming home today, and probably won't see him again for years, if ever." The ache grew too intense at the thought.

How had she fallen so hard for him? Had she succumbed to something as shallow as his charm? Maybe.

But she couldn't stop thinking about all she had shared with him—the passion, the laughter, the fun. The history. The tenderness.

She wouldn't hurt him by pursuing this investigation. She'd rather hurt herself. Which meant she'd better hit the road and never look back.

"Okay, Sis," Meg relented, "you're officially off the case. But would you mind stopping by the Tierneys' house and smoothing things over for me? I know Agnes will be disappointed. After your first meeting with her, she called me and told me how much she liked you. And Grant won't appreciate the delay. Tell them that some emergency came up."

"I won't lie, Meg. But I will apologize, and assure them that whoever you hire to replace me will do a much better job."

"Thanks. And Callie, if you need me, just call. I can be there in a flash, okay?"

After repeating vague reassurances, Callie murmured goodbye and called the Tierneys. Agnes answered, and Callie asked if she could drop by for a visit. Delighted with the prospect of company, Agnes invited her over for a light brunch.

Callie packed her luggage and carried her suitcases to the car. But as she went to unlock the door, which she swore she had locked last night, she found it open. And when she glanced on the front floorboard, she saw that her briefcase was missing.

Someone had stolen her briefcase...along with all the "dirt" she'd gathered against Jack Forrester.

CALLIE REPORTED THE THEFT to the deputy on duty at the sheriff's office that Sunday morning, but she held out little hope of having the briefcase found. The thief had left other valuables behind, including her cell phone and Meg's expensive CD player. Whoever had taken the briefcase had wanted only its contents.

Who?

A misguided friend of Jack's, she supposed. Someone in the community determined to save him from an unjust charge. Surely *not* one of the friends they had in common. Jimbo, Robbie, Frankie or any of the Forresters would never steal from her.

Thoroughly sick of this case and all its disturbing questions, Callie was glad she'd quit. Glad that she'd be leaving. She wore jeans and a soft, butter-yellow T-shirt instead of business clothes for brunch at the Tierneys. She intended to be comfortable during her drive to Tallahassee, as well as get the point across to Grant that her business with him had been concluded.

Agnes met her at the door with a smile, her flowing teal gown wafting around her. "I didn't have the chance to share my good news with you yesterday. Bob and I are getting married!"

"Oh, Agnes, that's wonderful." Callie hugged her, happy that she would have a man in her life other than Grant.

"My, don't you look pretty. You have such a nice figure, dear. You should wear jeans more often. I don't believe I've ever seen you in them before."

Callie had to smile. She'd spent her entire childhood in jeans. She supposed she'd come full circle.

Agnes peered closely into her face. "I see you smiling, but I sense you're feeling down. You're having man problems, aren't you? I can always tell."

"No!" Callie forced a little laugh. "No man problems. If I seem a little down, it's only because I have some news to break that you might not like."

"You're not leaving the Point, are you?"

"Actually, yes."

"But you've hardly had time to get to know Grant! I understand he arrived at the picnic quite late. Long after Bob and I had already left."

"Grant *is* here, isn't he?"

"Yes. He'll meet us in the solarium. But first, come with me." She hooked her arm around Callie's and ushered her into a plush bedroom decorated in tapestries and silk screens. "When you're having man problems, sometimes you need the right scent."

Agnes selected an ornate, emerald-green bottle from the top of her dresser. "This musk worked wonders on Bob. It magnifies a woman's natural pheromones. If a man is meant to notice you, he won't be able to resist you." With a dramatic flair, she uncorked the bottle. A musty, herbal smell permeated the room.

When she tipped the bottle to catch some in her hand, though, nothing came out.

Agnes frowned and stared into the bottle. "That's odd. I only used it once, and now it's gone!"

Callie murmured her thanks for the kind intention, hiding her relief that she wouldn't have to wear the musk. The scent was too cloying for her taste. Besides, she had no desire to magnify her pheromones. Her only "man problems" involved a soul-deep ache at leaving a certain golden-haired doctor behind.

Agnes, however, apparently meant to make a last-ditch effort at matching her up with Grant. After ushering Callie to the solarium, where wide, sunny windows overlooked the sea and lush plants thrived in every corner, she gestured to a table set for two with ruby-and-gold china, crystal goblets and a bottle of wine. "Dandelion wine," Agnes informed her. "I made it myself. I bring out a bottle now and then for special occasions."

"Agnes, why are there only two place settings?"

"I've already eaten. And I have friends to call about my engagement. I won't be able to join you and Grant."

"Ah, the lovely Miss Callie Marshall. Good morning."

Grant strolled into the solarium wearing a light blue oxford shirt that accentuated the startling azure of his eyes. He pulled out a chair for her and she reluctantly sat. "I hope you're well rested after all that dancing last night."

Callie's cheeks warmed as she remembered the awkward scene on the dance floor.

"Oh, did you two dance together?" inquired Agnes, her mauve brows arching into two happy question marks.

"No. Someday, hopefully." Grant settled into his chair and held her gaze with a fair emulation of sensual warmth.

She thought she might be sick. Deciding to get down to business before he could utter more nonsense, she said, "I wanted to tell you both that I'm withdrawing from the investigation."

"Withdrawing?" Agnes cried. "But why?"

"I'm afraid that my personal relationships with people in the community have made it difficult for me to run the investigation. I grew up on the Point. I believe you'll be better served by an investigator who didn't."

"Mother," Grant said in his silky-smooth voice, "don't you have phone calls to make?" Agnes murmured in agreement and gracefully glided from the room. Grant then smiled at Callie, uncorked the bottle of wine and filled her glass with a pale, flowery-scented liquid. "He got to you, didn't he?"

"I beg your pardon?"

"Forrester is a smooth operator when it comes to women."

Callie ignored the wine he'd poured for her and concentrated on concealing her resentment and pain. "Funny. He says the same about you."

"He would. He's never forgiven me for marrying his sister. Never thought I was good enough. He did everything he could to break up our marriage, and he finally succeeded."

She certainly hadn't heard that version of it.

Grant handed her a plate of chicken salad sandwiches, and after she'd taken one, he helped himself to a few. "Forrester then made it a point to intrude into every relationship of mine that he could. He stole my fiancé away from me. Did he tell you that? I believe he's quite proud of it. He didn't really want her for himself, of course. Lost interest in her as soon as I did." Grant shrugged. "It's an obsession with him, this need to...foil me. And he doesn't care whom he has to use to do it." He spooned melon balls onto his plate. "That includes you."

Although she'd been tormented by the suspicion that Jack's determination to "foil" Grant had motivated his pursuit of her—whether Jack consciously realized it or not—she didn't like hearing Grant say it. "It's really a moot point. I'm withdrawing from the case and leaving the Point today."

"I'd prefer you didn't withdraw from the case."

"Meg will hire another investigator who will do a much better job."

"Do you intend to submit your findings to Meg?"

For the moment, she felt almost glad that her briefcase had been stolen. "I'm sorry. That's impossible. Someone took my briefcase from my car last night. It contained all my research."

Grant frowned and narrowed his eyes at her.

"I hadn't found anything pertinent to the case, anyway."

"You realize who was behind the theft, don't you?"

She knew, of course, whom he meant.

"Answer that question as an investigator, Ms. Marshall—not as a woman who's been dazzled by a master manipulator."

Squaring her jaw in an attempt to rein in her rising temper, she reminded herself that she'd come here at Meg's request, to smooth things over. "If you're trying to blame Dr. Forrester, you'll need proof, or you may be opening yourself up to slander charges, or defamation of character."

"You know damn well he took it, or had someone take it."

"Someone may have stolen it in a misguided attempt to help him, but I'm sure that Dr. Forrester had nothing to do with it."

Grant let out a short, brutal laugh. "He got to you more than I thought he did." He sat back in his chair and inclined his head. "You know, I have considerable influence in the business world. I can help your career—and your sister's—beyond your wildest dreams." The calculation in his gaze sent a shiver down her back. "And I can destroy them both, too."

Oh Meg, I'm so sorry! She'd done her sister's cause more harm than good with her visit. "That's not a threat, is it?"

"Of course not. Just a fact." He leaned forward and handed her another tray. "Dewberry muffin?"

The doorbell chimed.

Grant called out, "Will you answer the door, Mother? And lead our guest in here to join us, please."

A terrible foreboding curled through Callie. "Guest?"

Grant broke open a muffin and buttered it. "I believe we may be able to settle this lawsuit right now."

Agnes's warm greeting rang from the other room, followed by a man's terse reply. Callie recognized the voice. Jack's.

"Amazing how quickly he accepted my invitation," Grant remarked, setting his buttered muffin halves aside. "All I had to do was call and say that I, uh, had you here." He held up his wineglass in a toast. "I do find you to be an invaluable asset."

With a sickening plunge of her heart, Callie realized this would be another showdown between Grant and Jack, and that she'd been used as a pawn again—or a trophy. Jack would find her here having a cozy breakfast with his enemy, and Grant would gloat.

"What are you planning to do?" she demanded.

"Offer him a settlement. If he doesn't take it, I'm ready to use the Sharon Landers case to my best advantage. I can be very creative. The jury will be ready to bury him alive."

Callie stared at him in horror. He *had* overheard Frankie. And now Jack would pay the price, one way or another.

Agnes fluttered near the solarium entrance, waving her teal-draped arms in welcoming gestures, her face beaming beneath her bright red hair, her murmurs clearly indicating her pleasure at another guest's arrival.

She then receded from sight, and Jack appeared in the archway of the solarium, his shoulders taut, his beard-shadowed jaw hardened. He wore the same white shirt and jeans he had last night. It appeared he hadn't been to bed. She wondered why.

His gaze went immediately to Callie, as if to make sure she was okay, as if he'd expected to find her bound and gagged.

Despite all the reasons that had kept her from meeting him last night and the panic that had sent her packing this morning, her heart clamored as their gazes locked. She wanted to rush into his arms, kiss the tension from his face and declare herself firmly on "his side."

Which would be tantamount to professional *and* emotional self-destruction. She had to leave, as soon as possible, before she threw all logical and ethical considerations to the wind.

But Jack stood between her and the door, so she remained tensely seated. His gaze shifted from her and took in the table set for two, the flowers, the wine. A muscle flexed in his jaw, and he leveled a cold, hard stare at Grant.

"Good morning, Mr. Forrester." If not for the malice in Grant's gaze and his withholding of Jack's proper title, Callie could believe he was welcoming a friend. "Please, have a seat."

Jack remained standing. The animosity between the two men almost crackled in the air with electric tension. Did anything matter to them more than besting the other? "What the hell do you want, Tierney?"

"That just happens to be the theme of our little party. I'm ready to cut you a deal—to drop the lawsuit and put the whole nasty business behind us—*if* you're willing to accept my terms. In writing. Here and now."

Callie's breath caught. She fervently wished that they *would* put "the whole nasty business" behind them. But she knew that Grant's demands would be unjust, and that Jack wouldn't consider bowing to them.

Instead of telling Grant to go to hell, Jack surprisingly turned his gaze to her. "I want to talk to you, Callie. In private."

Her pulse beat in her throat like the wings of a trapped dove. She couldn't talk to him in private, or she'd be lost. She'd tell him she loved him, and that she'd stand beside him forever and fight to the death for his honor.

She had to leave. *Now.*

"No, I'm sorry, Jack." She set her napkin beside her plate and forced her gaze to Grant. "As a matter of fact, I really must be going. I have a long drive to Tallahassee." She rose and strode from the table, avoiding Jack's eyes as she shouldered past him.

His arm shot around her waist, barring her way. She

looked at him with a sense of panic, ready to break from his hold and run. "I don't know what terms he's talking about," he said in a harsh undertone, "or why he thinks I'd settle." His gaze searched hers with an earnestness that brought a lump to her throat. "But I'm going to leave it up to you, Callie. You tell me what you want me to do about this damn lawsuit, and I'll do it. In writing. Here and now."

Stunned beyond words, she stared at him. He couldn't mean it! And yet, she believed he did. He would settle with his worst enemy, despite the weakness of Grant's case, despite the damage to his own career. He'd agree to *any* terms. "Why?"

"Because nothing is as important to me as you are," he heatedly whispered. "Nothing."

The love she'd tried so hard to extinguish overflowed from her heart to fill her chest, her throat, her eyes. She had no doubt that he meant it.

"I'm willing to drop the cash amount down to two hundred thousand," Grant coaxed, his hateful voice coming from some faraway world, "which your insurance company will gladly pay. Then, as a personal matter between us, you'll sign over the beach property at the end of the Point. And issue a public apology."

A muscle contracted in Jack's jaw, but his gaze remained on Callie.

"Oh, God, Jack." She didn't want him to settle at any price, but neither could she stand the thought of subjecting him to the pain of having the Sharon Landers case publicized. "There's something you need to know—"

"What my right-hand man is trying to tell you, Forrester," Grant interrupted, "is that we're ready to use our ammunition. She supplied me with a bundle of fascinating notes, taped testimony, and photos to show you in just the right light to the jury."

Callie sucked in an outraged breath. "My briefcase! *You* took it."

"My favorite submission," Grant continued, "is her report on the Sharon Landers case. You remember—the young mother you killed on your operating table."

Jack stiffened as if he'd been struck with a whip. Before Callie could utter a word, he swung a dazed stare to her.

"He's lying," she whispered.

The uncertainty in his pain-filled gaze cut deeply into her. How could he think she would betray him so callously?

Then again, why shouldn't he think it? She'd been warning him that she intended to gather "dirt" to ruin his name. She hadn't told him she'd withdrawn from the investigation, or that she'd had a change of heart.

Grant laughed and leaned back in his chair. "A man gets his money's worth with Callie Marshall. I've thoroughly enjoyed her services." He indulged in a sip of wine. "I'll have to keep her name in mind for the next time I want to *screw* somebody."

Jack lunged across the table at him, sending dishes crashing to the floor. The wineglass flew from Grant's hold as he tipped wildly back in his chair to evade the hand that went for his throat. Jack grabbed a fistful of his shirt instead and jerked him closer.

"No, Jack, no!" Callie hooked both arms around the one he'd drawn back for a punch. "He'll have you arrested!"

"What the Sam Hill is going on here?"

The stern voice of Sheriff Gallagher froze them all in surprise. The stalwart lawman stood frowning in the solarium's arched doorway, the morning sunlight glinting off his badge.

Agnes hovered behind him, wide-eyed. "Oh, my. Oh, my!"

With clear reluctance, Jack let go of his grip on Grant's shirt and lowered his fist. Callie released his arm, and Grant pushed himself up from the table where he'd been dragged across his plate.

Flicking crumbs and mashed melon balls from his shirt, he murmured, "What took you so long, Sheriff? I told you he'd cause a disturbance. He assaulted me in my own home."

The sheriff glowered at Grant. "There ought to be a law against baiting a man the way you bait Doc Forrester, but as far as I know, there ain't." He then turned his glare to Jack. "And you should have better sense than to let him rile you into violence."

"He didn't hit him," Callie stated. "He just grabbed his shirt. That's all. I'm a witness."

The sheriff surprised her with a quelling frown. "Tierney told me you suspect that Doc stole your briefcase. Do you have any grounds to support that charge?"

Callie's mouth dropped open, and Jack leveled another stare at her. "I never suspected him!" She shot Grant a furious glare. "You must have called the sheriff before I even told you my briefcase had been stolen."

"Check his car, Sheriff," Grant demanded. "I bet you'll find her briefcase in his car."

"I can't search his car without probable cause."

"Wait just a damn minute." Jack narrowed his eyes at Grant. "He's too cocksure about this to be taking a wild guess. I was out on my boat all night, which left him plenty of opportunity to plant something in my car."

Grant snorted. "He's already making up excuses. Sheriff, that briefcase contained material relevant to my lawsuit. If you don't search his car, I'll report you to higher authorities."

"Report me! For what?"

With a muttered curse, Jack brushed past Callie and the sheriff on his way to the door. "*I'll* search my damn car, and if I find anything that's not supposed to be there, Tierney, I'll make you sorry you ever tangled with me."

"Sheriff, did you hear that threat?" Grant trailed after Jack. "Come along, Mother. I may need an honest witness."

The sheriff grumbled beneath his breath, and everyone filed outside to Jack's gleaming black sports car. It took Jack less than a minute to draw out Callie's briefcase from behind the seats.

"Aha!" Grant said, peering through the window. "I knew you'd stolen that briefcase. Sheriff, I see something else rather suspicious behind those seats, too."

Barely sparing the briefcase a glance, Jack tossed it to Callie. The briefcase was empty. She had no doubt that Grant Tierney had taken its contents before planting it in Jack's car.

Jack then pulled out another item from behind the seats. Rising to stand beside his car, he held up a plastic bag that contained a small vial of reddish-brown liquid. "What the hell is this, Tierney?"

"That's a good question." Grant looked a little too smug. "Sheriff, you'd better take a closer look at whatever substance Dr. Forrester had in his car. I wouldn't doubt it's some kind of hallucinogen, like the one he injected into my mother."

As the insinuation sank in, Jack's mouth twisted in anger and he started toward Grant.

The sheriff laid a restraining hand on Jack's arm. "I have no right to confiscate anything from Doc unless I have reason to believe it's an illegal substance, which I don't."

"Then my attorney will be serving you with a subpoena, Sheriff. The jury will need to know that he was caught carrying around hallucinogens in his car."

Jack handed the bag to the sheriff. "I'd like this substance analyzed, and if it's some form of hallucinogen, I want him arrested for planting it in my car."

"You'd better be able to prove that allegation, Forrester," Grant snarled, "since you've publicly maligned my character."

"You boys are a pain in the butt," the sheriff muttered. With a frown, he removed the vial from the bag and held the slim, liquid-filled tube up to the sunlight. "I don't know what it could possibly be." He opened the vial. A musty fragrance wafted in the warm, noonday air.

"I recognize that smell!" Callie declared. "Don't you, Agnes?"

"No, she doesn't," snapped Grant. "And I think I'd better have that stuff analyzed myself." His hand shot out and snatched the open vial from the sheriff.

"Hey!" The sheriff reached to grab it back.

As Grant jerked the vial out of his reach, the liquid streamed out and splashed across his face. He gasped, shut his eyes, dropped the vial and frantically wiped at the reddish-brown rivulets with his hands and sleeves. The vial, meanwhile, fell into the grass.

Cursing beneath his breath, the sheriff reached for it.

Jack stopped him. "Scoop it up into this." He handed him the plastic bag. "Don't get the liquid on your skin. Who the hell knows what it is?"

Squinting and blinking, Grant made a move toward the sheriff. Jack blocked his way, glowering at him, as the sheriff carefully scooped the now half-empty vial into the plastic bag.

"I *do* recognize the smell," Agnes declared. "It smells exactly like my pheromone enhancer."

"Don't say another word, Mother," Grant thundered.

"Don't yell at her," Jack warned.

Grant's face, which he'd dried with his shirtsleeves, was now mottled red. "I think it's time you got the hell off my property, Forrester."

"Agnes," said Callie as the two men glared at each other, "did you use your pheromone enhancer on the Fourth of July?"

"Ms. Marshall, if you say another word, I'll sue you along with Forrester," Grant threatened, his face now seriously splotchy and his voice sounding oddly hoarse. "I'll sue Meg, too, and her senior partners."

"I *did* use it on the Fourth of July," Agnes recalled as the sheriff walked to his car with the bagged vial. "I rubbed just a little on my pulse points. I was determined to make Bob notice me at the picnic. It worked, too. Very well. Remember, Grant? I tried to get you to use some. It enhances men's pheromones as well as women's. My good friend in India made it for me during my last trip there. She used a special blend of herbs and mushrooms. But how did my pheromone enhancer get in Jack's car?"

"My face," Grant rasped. He'd turned a peculiar

shade of pale, making the splotches stand out all the more. "It's numb."

"Oh, my!" Agnes peered at him in wide-eyed concern. "It looks like he's having an allergic reaction. He has them worse than I do." A realization hit her, and her mouth opened into an O shape. "Do you think something in the pheromone enhancer caused my allergic reaction at the picnic?"

"I'd say that's a real good guess," Jack replied. "And if it was made with the kind of mushrooms and herbs I suspect it was, the musk probably caused your hallucinations, too. Especially if you rubbed it into your 'pulse points.'"

Grant wheezed and clutched his chest.

Jack took a step closer, looking thoroughly annoyed. "Is your throat closing up?" he demanded brusquely.

Grant gasped and staggered backward, visibly straining for every breath. "Stay away!" he croaked. "Don't touch me. Mother...call...ambulance."

Agnes cast a frightened, confused glance at Jack, who nodded his encouragement. With a little cry, she hurried up the stairway and into her house. Grant, meanwhile, clawed at his throat and broke out into a sweat. The sheriff pulled out his radio and spoke into it.

Jack cursed and walked to his car.

Callie hovered anxiously beside Grant as he leaned against his own car and gasped for breath. His eyes, mouth and chin had swollen to an incredible puffiness, distorting his face. "Jack," she cried, "an ambulance won't get here in time!"

Jack was already striding back from the car with his emergency kit under one arm as he peeled away the plastic wrap from a prepackaged hypodermic syringe. "He's going into anaphylactic shock."

Grant slumped over onto Callie, and she struggled beneath his weight. "He stopped breathing!" The sheriff hurried to her aid and lowered the unconscious man onto the concrete driveway. Thoroughly frightened, Callie knelt over him and pressed her mouth to his, administering mouth-to-mouth resuscitation. While she did, Jack injected medication into Grant's arm. "This might not work fast enough," he said. "Let me see if air is moving through his lungs." Callie moved aside, and Jack listened through a stethoscope to Grant's chest and throat. "Sheriff, do you have a ballpoint pen?"

The sheriff grunted a yes and pulled one from his pocket.

Jack directed him to take it apart and hand him the empty bottom tube. "Callie, find the alcohol swab." As he spoke in calm, authoritative tones, he reached into his emergency kit and brought out a shiny implement, which opened into a glinting knife. "Tierney, if you can hear me, try to understand what I'm saying. I'm going to open an emergency airway so you can breathe. If I don't, you'll suffocate."

With a dull sense of horror, Callie realized that Jack meant to slice open his throat.

"Callie," Jack murmured, his gaze intently focused on Grant, "you might not want to watch." He took the alcohol swab from her trembling fingers, cleaned off the blade, swabbed the skin near the base of Grant's throat and cut a short, vertical incision.

As a neat, crimson line blossomed around the incision, she lifted her eyes to Jack's face—not because of the blood or the slight faintness it had caused, but because of an almost spiritual awe dawning in her.

She'd always loved him, but she'd never seen him in quite this light before. He worked with intense concentration and smooth, precise moves, and she knew he expended the same care he would give to the most valued person in his life. Yet he was working on his enemy, a man who had scarred him, slandered him and schemed to rob him of his property and career. A man who could possibly sue him for the work he now performed.

And he did this lifesaving work on his adversary not because of some legal consequence that could be levied against him if he didn't, or because of a sense of duty, or even for Agnes's sake. He did it, Callie knew, because of an innate goodness. He would do everything he could, endure whatever he must, to prevent the death or grievous suffering of a fellow human being.

He was a strong, bright, positive force that would illuminate any darkness. The people lucky enough to claim a place in his heart could count on him through any crisis, physical or emotional.

How could she *not* love him? How could she *not* want him as a vital, integral part of her life?

A siren grew steadily louder until an ambulance pulled into the driveway. Jack glanced up from his work, and his gaze collided with Callie's. He looked surprised to find her watching him—or maybe surprised at the intensity of her stare.

A shout from the ambulance driver claimed his attention, and Jack apprised him of the situation. Callie realized that an open tube protruded from a neat, white bandage around Grant's throat. Though his face remained swollen and mottled, his chest moved rhythmically and his glazed, bloodshot eyes had opened.

Jack had saved his life.

Although she'd had no doubt that he would, a huge, hot ball of emotion rose in Callie's throat and made her eyes burn. Voices babbled around her as the emergency crew asked Agnes and Jack questions, the sheriff talked to his deputy who had just arrived, and Grant rasped incoherent protests to the paramedics who lifted him onto a stretcher.

Through it all, Callie couldn't draw her gaze away from the tall, strong, golden-haired doctor at the heart of the activity. There was so much she needed to tell him. She couldn't forget the doubt in his eyes when Grant had mentioned the Sharon Landers case. She couldn't bear to have him believe for even a moment longer that she'd submitted that information.

Jack turned to listen to something Agnes was saying, and his gaze again met Callie's. Before Callie could glean any hint of how he felt about her now, Agnes pulled him into a hearty hug.

"You saved my son's life," she cried, "just like you saved mine. I'll never be able to thank you enough. I don't care what he says—I'm dropping that lawsuit. Now that Bob and I are getting married, I won't have to live with Grant anymore."

"Excuse me, Ms. Agnes." The sheriff lumbered up beside her. "Would you mind giving me the rest of your, uh, fairy-moan stuff? I'd like to take a close look at it."

"I'll give you the bottle, but it's empty. Someone drained it." In a loud whisper, she theorized, "I believe it was Grant. He didn't want me dating Bob. But after I used it that one time, I didn't *need* any more of the pheromone enhancer."

"I'll take the bottle, please, ma'am," the sheriff said. As Agnes led him up the steps and into the house, a raspy cry came from the stretcher. One of the paramedics bent to listen. "He's talking about snakes coming at him. Purple dragon snakes." The young man listened awhile longer, then glanced at Jack. "He says you sent them, Doc, and that he's going to sue you for everything you've got."

"Guess I'd better be careful, then, or I'll be finding purple dragon snakes in my car."

The paramedic exchanged a droll glance with him and carried the stretcher to the ambulance. The driver called out, "You coming with us, Doc?"

"Hell, no. He's all yours."

The ambulance pulled out of the driveway. Callie came to stand beside Jack as he watched the ambulance speed away. "I've always wanted to slit his throat," he muttered. "Somehow this wasn't the way I pictured it."

Callie bit her lip with a wry smile. At least he'd managed to hold the comment until they were alone. "So he knew from the beginning what had caused her hallucinations, didn't he?"

Jack glanced at her as if he hadn't realized anyone stood beside him. "Of course he knew. She told him she'd used her 'pheromone enhancer,' and probably explained that it was made from herbs and mushrooms by her friend in India. Wouldn't that tip *you* off?"

"Of course." Callie pondered that for a moment, then shook her head at Grant's deceit. "He planted it in your car to make a jury believe you carry hallucinogens around with you."

"That's right. I would have lost all credibility."

She glanced at him anxiously. "Do you think he'll try to cause you more trouble?"

"I doubt it. He'll have too many other things on his mind. After he'd caused Becky so many problems, I hired an investigator to keep an eye on him. We came up with a few leads that interested the FBI. Seems that Tierney's been involved in quite a few shady real estate dealings. I believe the feds will have enough to put him away for a long time."

Now that she fully understood Grant's unscrupulous nature, Callie didn't find that surprising at all. And she didn't waste her time thinking about it.

The troubling uncertainty she'd noticed before had returned to Jack's gaze, and the silence that fell between them suddenly felt awkward. Nothing seemed as important as answering the questions he wasn't asking her.

"Can we go somewhere private to talk?" she asked.

He gestured toward a wooded pathway that ran between Tierney's property and his. Callie knew from her childhood that the path led to a pier over the beach. Silently she preceded him through a fragrant thicket of cedars, oaks and palms, her heart aching at the continued awkwardness between them.

The shady coolness of the woods soon gave way to hot, hazy sunshine as they traipsed between swaying sea oats and mountainous sand dunes, then onto the weathered, wooden planks of the pier. Tumultuous gray-green waves crested into whitecaps on either side of them until they reached the very end of the pier, where the water was deeper and swells rolled in majestic silence.

Callie lifted her face to the salty gulf breeze and inhaled the fortifying tang of the sea before she turned to face Jack. His shaggy golden hair glimmered and danced in the wind, but his dark-eyed gaze remained sober and watchful.

How many times had they fished from this pier together, or swum, or shoved each other in? Countless times, and never had a silence intruded as heavily as this one.

"Jack, I'm sorry that I ever got involved in this investigation." She leaned against the end rail, and he leaned against the side one. "I shouldn't have."

He lifted a shoulder in a shrug but didn't comment.

"I called Meg this morning," she continued, desperately missing his smile, "and withdrew from the investigation."

He inclined his head and stared at her. "So your breakfast with Tierney was purely social?"

"No! I'd promised Meg that I'd stop by and explain my reason for withdrawing from the case."

"Which was…?"

Her throat tightened with emotion. "I, uh, lost my objectivity."

He pursed his mouth and gazed out at the sea.

"Jack, please believe that I never gave Tierney anything. Anything at all! Especially not a report about Sharon Landers."

He frowned and swung his gaze back to hers. "Did you think I believed him?"

"Didn't you?"

"No." They stared at each other in bemusement. "Call me naive or egotistical or thickheaded," he said, "but I just can't bring myself to believe that you would knowingly hurt me."

The emotion that had clogged her throat now throbbed with renewed pressure. "But when Grant said I turned in that report, I saw the question in your eyes."

"If a question came into my eyes, Callie, it was when he said I killed a young mother on my operating table, and you said he was lying. As much as I appreciated the blind defense, I won't deny the truth."

She gaped at him, stunned by the raw pain in his expression, and even more by the reason for it. "The truth? What are you calling 'the truth'?"

"Tierney might have worded it a little harshly, but Sharon Landers *was* a patient of mine. A young mother. And she did die on my operating table. I wasn't sure if you knew that, or how you'd feel about me once you did."

"Oh, Jack, the mistake wasn't yours, and even if it had been, it wouldn't change the way I feel about you."

He stared at her for a long, fierce moment, then blew out a harsh breath he'd meant as a laugh.

"I've never been more unsure of how anybody felt about me, Callie. You sent me a message to never contact you again, and you planned to leave without a goodbye. But then the whole time I performed that tracheotomy on Tierney, you stared at me like I was some kind of hero. And now you're looking at me with the kind of warmth I've been waiting forever to see in your eyes."

That warmth intensified into a bright, beautiful flame, and an unbearable anguish filled him. "Damn it, Callie, no matter how much I want to keep you here, you've got to understand that I'm no hero. What I did back there was a simple emergency procedure that anyone could do. Tierney didn't die, but Sharon Landers did, and I can't guarantee that my next patient won't die, too. I don't know which is worse—having you scorn me as a negligent quack, or revere me as some infallible medical god."

She recoiled slightly, as if he'd wounded her. "I don't think of you as either one. And I'm sorry that I confused you. I've been confused myself."

He'd known that. He also knew that in her confusion, she'd built him up into something he wasn't. He ransacked his mind, his heart, for a way to explain his fear that when the inevitable day came and he fell short of the hero he saw reflected in her gaze, her warmth would cool, and though she would never deliberately hurt him, he would lose her in the most final of ways.

He reached deep for words to explain, but found instead only a painfully chaotic need.

"Jack," she whispered, laying her palms against his face with infinite tenderness. "It's me. Callie."

And before he could tame the chaos or mask the need, she did what only Callie could do. She peered through it all with her luminous gray-green eyes and connected with him. Tapped directly into his psyche. Bound him to her with a sharing so deep and steeped in time that fear and doubt lost all power.

He could be, would be, whatever she needed. Always.

"I love you, Cal."

"I love you, too, Jack." Slowly, softly, she kissed him.

He pulled her against him and kissed her until the sweet, hot joy coursing through him combusted into a deeper yearning. "I want to marry you, Callie," he proclaimed in a gruff, drawn-out whisper against her ear.

She drew back with a heated, intimate smile. "You do?"

"Yeah."

Playfulness mixed with the heat in her gaze and put him on his guard. "Tell you what." She brushed her mouth lightly across his. "Let's play the game you mentioned the other night. I think you called it, 'Please, Jack, please, make love to me.'"

His body hardened at the very suggestion, and he couldn't help cradling her slim, jean-clad hips to his and capturing her mouth in a hard, possessive kiss. "You did notice that I asked you to marry me," he eventually whispered, "didn't you?"

"I'm getting to that." She raked her fingers through his hair, smiled into his eyes and nipped at his bottom lip. "If you win the game, I have to marry you."

He stared at her, unsure whether or not he should be happy about the proposition. The game itself was a brilliant idea, of course. Truly inspired. But... "What if *you* win?"

"Then *you* have to marry *me*."

He continued to stare, thoroughly amazed. Just when he thought he couldn't possibly love her more, she proved him wrong again. "You realize that since it's my game," he cautioned, "I get to set the rules."

"Fair enough."

Although it took them awhile and a few dozen distracting kisses, they actually managed to reach his house and lock the doors before the game officially started.

Their first round required a rematch. So did the second. The third had a clear winner, but a formal protest was lodged....

Heart of the West

A brand-new Harlequin continuity series
begins in July 1999
with

Husband for Hire
by
Susan Wiggs

*Beautician Twyla McCabe was Dear Abby
with a blow-dryer, listening to everyone else's
troubles. But now her well-meaning customers
have gone too far. No way was she attending
the Hell Creek High School Reunion with Rob
Carter, M.D. Who would believe a woman
who dyed hair for a living could be engaged
to such a hunk?*

Here's a preview!

magnitude of what that passion meant.

CHAPTER ONE

"THIS ISN'T FOR the masquerade. This is for me."

"What's for you?"

"This."

Rob didn't move fast, but with a straightforward deliberation she found oddly thrilling. He gripped Twyla by the upper arms and pulled her to him, covering her mouth with his.

Dear God, a kiss. She couldn't remember the last time a man had kissed her. And what a kiss. It was everything a kiss should be—sweet, flavored with strawberries and wine and driven by an underlying passion that she felt surging up through him, creating an answering need in her. She rested her hands on his shoulders and let her mouth soften, open. He felt wonderful beneath her hands, his muscles firm, his skin warm, his mouth... She just wanted to drown in him, drown in the passion. If he was faking his ardor, he was damned good. When he stopped kissing her, she stepped back. Her disbelieving fingers went to her mouth, lightly touching her moist, swollen lips.

"That...wasn't in the notes," she objected weakly.

"I like to ad-lib every once in a while."

"I need to sit down." Walking backward, never taking her eyes off him, she groped behind her and found the Adirondack-style porch swing. *Get a grip,* she told herself. *It was only a kiss.*

"I think," he said mildly, "it's time you told me just why you were so reluctant to come back here for the reunion."

"And why I had to bring a fake fiancé as a shield?"

Very casually, he draped his arm along the back of the porch swing. "I'm all ears, Twyla. Why'd I have to practically hog-tie you to get you back here?"

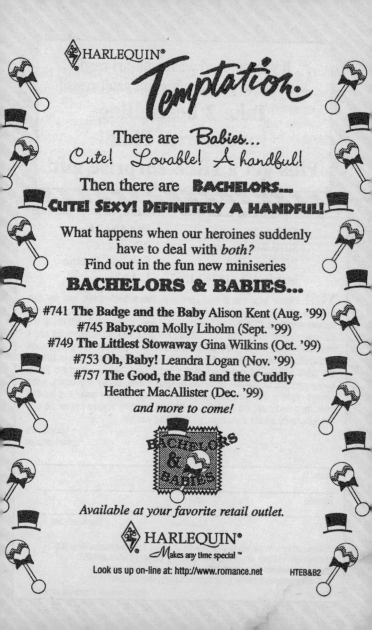

Temptation®

COMING NEXT MONTH